THE INDIAN FIGHTER'S RETURN

In Memory
of
Louis A. King

THE INDIAN FIGHTER'S RETURN

Jack Cummings

Chivers Press • G.K. Hall & Co.
Bath, Avon, England   Thorndike, Maine USA

This Large Print edition is published by Chivers Press, England, and by G.K. Hall & Co., USA.

Published in 1995 in the U.K. by arrangement with the author.

Published in 1994 in the U.S. by arrangement with Walker Publishing Company, Inc.

U.K. Hardcover ISBN 0–7451–2374–0 (Chivers Large Print)
U.S. Softcover   ISBN 0–8161–5991–2 (Nightingale Series Edition)

All the characters and events portrayed in this work are fictitious.

The text of this Large Print edition is unabridged.
Other aspects of the book may vary from the original edition.

Set in 16pt New Times Roman.

Printed in the U.K. on acid-free paper.

British Library Cataloguing in Publication Data available

Library of Congress Cataloging-in-Publication Data

Cummings, Jack, 1925–
    The Indian fighter's return / Jack Cummings.
       p.   cm.
    ISBN 0–8161–5991–2 (alk. paper : lg. print)
    1. Large type books.   I. Title.
[PS3553.U444I5   1994]
813'.54—dc20   94–9341

CHAPTER ONE

Silver City, Owyhee County, Idaho, July 1892

Over the years, the town had boomed and receded and boomed again with the vagaries of its gold and silver mines. The population varied with these cycles, but Silver City remained the seat of Owyhee County.

There were two hotels, the Idaho and the War Eagle, six general stores, two hardware stores, four restaurants, a photographer's gallery, three barbershops, a newspaper, four lawyers, two doctors, three churches, eight saloons, and the county courthouse.

Now, tacked up or pasted onto many of these board buildings were the election posters of two rival candidates for the office of sheriff, vacated by the recent death of the incumbent.

One candidate, a former deputy, James J. Halloran, had been chosen by the town council to fill the position until a vote could be taken.

The other was his challenger, famed former Indian fighter and ex-Army scout Jon Seaver. Broke and unemployed, he had no law enforcement experience, but hoped to parlay his Indian-fighting reputation into an election victory.

Seaver stood staring out the open door of his rented campaign office, squinting at the sun

1

glare on the dusty street. Fifteen years, he was thinking. Fifteen years since he'd scouted, at the age of twenty, for General Howard's vastly superior army force that pursued Chief Joseph and his fleeing Nez Percé up a 1700-mile trail through Idaho Territory.

And fifteen years since his famous hand-to-hand killing of a defiant Nez Percé chieftain named Broken Horn, an exaggerated account of which had become a legend in the West.

Now the Indian wars were over, ended with the catastrophe at Wounded Knee, and he was out of a job.

So he had returned to the territory where the incident of his initial fame had first caught the public fancy, and where, by lucky coincidence, the job of county sheriff was up for grabs.

*   *   *

The doorway darkened abruptly, blocked by the corpulent figure of young Ray Warden, local businessman and Seaver's volunteer campaign manager. Agitation showed on Warden's face.

'We've got a problem,' Warden said.

Seaver's lean, tanned features squinted in a frown. 'Well?'

'Ella Gordon just got off the stage and went into the Idaho Hotel.'

'Who the hell is Ella Gordon?'

'You don't know?'

2

'I'm asking.'

'Ella Gordon,' Warden said, 'is just about the best-known woman activist and lecturer against government mistreatment of Indians in these parts.'

'What's she doing here?'

'I don't know yet. But if I was to guess, I don't think I'd be happy.'

'Why do you say that?'

'Look,' Warden said, 'to put it bluntly, Ella Gordon is an Indian lover, pure and simple.'

'I reckon that's her privilege.'

'Sure,' Warden said. 'The problem is if she is also an Indian-fighter hater.'

Seaver was silent, then said, 'Meaning me, I guess.'

'Meaning you.'

'So?'

'What if she's come here to talk against you?'

'Let her talk,' Seaver said. 'I've faced worse odds in my time.'

'Not like her, you haven't.'

'You've heard her speak?'

Warden nodded. 'A lecture, one time down in Winnemucca, Nevada. She was haranguing a bunch of cattlemen about treatment of Paiutes they'd hired as buckaroos.'

'Not a receptive audience, I'd bet.'

'Not at first. But believe it or not, she ended up with about half those old boys won over.' He paused. 'A very handsome woman, Jon, and that has its effect, too. She cuts an

3

appealing figure.'

'Maybe I ought to call on her,' Seaver said.

Warden hesitated, then said, 'She's an educated lady, Jon. Out of some Eastern finishing school, I understand, before she found this Indian cause to espouse.'

'So?'

'Well, you're cut a little on the rough side,' Warden said. 'If you go calling, be on your good behavior—don't go antagonizing her more than she might already be. Keep in mind you're trying to win an election.'

'I'm not likely to forget that.'

'I hope not. You're running on old fame against an incumbent with actual law enforcement experience that you don't have. You can't afford to lose a single vote.'

'This isn't Wyoming,' Seaver said. 'Women don't have the vote here yet. And I'd guess her audiences are mostly women.'

'Didn't I tell you how this woman can influence men,' Warden said, 'as well as women? And, believe me, wives can turn husbands against anybody they don't favor.'

'I wouldn't know about that. I've always been a bachelor.'

'Well, I haven't,' Warden said. 'And I'm telling you how it is.'

'All right. You've told me. What do you suggest I do?'

'Let me contact her first,' Warden said, 'and see for certain why she's come to town.'

4

'All right,' Seaver said. 'But remember I'll be in front of the public at two o'clock this afternoon. Scheduled to make a speech in front of the town hall.'

Warden looked at his watch. 'Gives me a couple of hours. Let's hope you're not the reason for her coming.'

Seaver nodded, but looked perplexed. 'I don't guess I ever met her kind before. Hell, I been made out the hero in more than one dime novel, as well as some half-true military accounts. That's what gave me the idea of running for office. Never heard much criticism before.'

'Times are changing, Jon,' Warden said. 'But even so, maybe I'm concerned about nothing. She may be here on a routine stop to elsewhere.'

'Let me know what you find out,' Seaver said. 'I can't see what she'd have against me.'

'No? Jon, you project an image of everything contrary to her cause. And, having heard her speak, I might say, Hell hath no fury like a woman with a cause!'

'Like that, eh?'

'Speaking is only part of it. She has a reputation as a writer too. A book citing wrongdoings by the government—and the army—against the poor redskins, going back a half-century or more. *Years of Dishonor*, I think it's called.'

Seaver shrugged. 'Well, talk to the lady. Like

you said, you might be mistaking her intentions.'

'Yeah, let's hope so,' Warden said, and went out the door.

*   *   *

Seaver sat at the old scarred desk he'd moved into his temporary office. He was bucking the odds, running against the acting sheriff, Big Jim Halloran, who had considerable backing among some of the Silver City mine promoters. Halloran was a born politician. All Seaver had going for him was his reputation; he was gambling that alone it would give him a fighting chance for the lawman job, one he needed badly.

He didn't need any additional opposition, that was sure.

Seaver had misled Warden by feigning ignorance of who Ella Gordon was. He *had* heard of her. Over the past few years she had become better known perhaps than he was. With most of the Indians now on the reservations, her fame was growing while his own was becoming a thing of the past.

How old was she? he wondered, then discarded the thought. What difference did it make?

*   *   *

An hour later, Warden came back. He wore a poker face, but said, 'Best you talk with her.'

'What happened?'

'My guess was right. She heard about your campaign and made it a priority to stop here.'

'To try to ruin my election bid?'

'I would assume so, seeing as how all I got from her was a long tirade against the Indian wars and those who took part in them.'

Seaver was on his feet now, anger showing on his face. 'Goddammit! She should have seen some of the redskin atrocities I've seen.'

Warden nodded and said, 'She agreed to hear your side of the story. Take advantage of that. Do it now, before she scuttles your next speech with one of her own.'

Seaver was already reaching for his hat. 'Wish me luck,' he said.

'Yeah,' Warden said. 'With her, you may damn well need it.'

*   *   *

Ella Gordon was waiting for him in the small lobby of the hotel.

Seaver noticed she was nearing thirty and, as Warden had said, a very handsome woman. Her attractiveness tempered his ire, but only slightly.

As he introduced himself, her response was cool. 'Yes, Mr Seaver, I'm well aware of who you are.'

'You don't seem too pleased to meet me, ma'am.'

'Do you know who I am?'

'I do, ma'am. I surely do.'

'Then you should know my feelings, Mr Seaver. Do you expect me to take pleasure in meeting a man best known for killing Indians?'

'I was a scout for the army, ma'am. Any killing I did came with the job I was hired to do.'

'You give that as an excuse?'

'No, ma'am. I state that as a fact.'

'It is my understanding you took part in the recent action at Wounded Knee,' she said.

He was surprised that she knew that. But he responded, 'I did.'

'And how many of the women and children there did you fire on, Mr Seaver?'

'None deliberately.'

'None deliberately,' she said. 'But many were killed.'

'The big Hotchkiss guns firing from the hill took many of them,' he said awkwardly. 'I had no control over that, ma'am.'

'Does it ease your conscience that you didn't?'

'My conscience? I was in a battle. A battle that maybe got out of hand. That's a thing that sometimes happened. In the heat of a fight, the confusion, and all.'

'A battle? It has been termed more frequently a massacre.'

8

'Well, ma'am, it has been my experience that a battle can sometimes turn quickly into a massacre. For one side or the other. There's been many a massacre committed by Injuns.'

She ignored this comment. 'You fought Indians for many years, Mr Seaver.'

'Yes, ma'am. Starting when I was eighteen.'

'And at twenty you achieved undying fame by killing a Nez Percé named Broken Horn.'

'You know more about me than I would have suspected,' he said.

'I was a young girl at the time. Attending a school in the East. But I followed, in *Harper's Weekly*, the account of Chief Joseph's flight northward under a running attack of the army—trying to reach sanctuary for his people in Canada.'

'Yes, ma'am.'

'And Chief Joseph's stirring words, at the end: "*I am tired; my heart is sick and sad. From where the sun now stands I will fight no more forever.*" The heartfelt pain in those words! It led me to become a defender of the rights of his kind.'

'He was a good man,' Seaver said.

'I'm shocked that you admit it!' she said. She paused. 'And Broken Horn, the one whom you killed in hand-to-hand combat, was he a good man, too?'

'Not for me, he wasn't. He caught mc off-guard as I was making a lone camp while scouting ahead of the troops. It was

9

him or me.'

'Him or you,' she said. 'Yes, I've heard those words before. Or to be more exact: them or us. Usually from some ranking army officer.'

'Because ma'am,' Seaver said, 'in most cases that's the way it was.'

'Indeed?'

'If you had ever been out there on a scene of battle, you would better understand.'

'Tell me, Mr Seaver, how can you possibly take such great pride in your reputation as an Indian killer?'

'I have never taken great pride in it, ma'am. The reputation was foisted on me by others. Foisted on me and exaggerated until I've sometimes had trouble recognizing who they're talking about.'

'Yet you are now flaunting that embellished reputation before the voters in an effort to get elected.'

'It's all I've got, ma'am, and I'm in need of a job. There's not much call for Indian-fighting army scouts nowadays.'

'Thank heaven for that!'

'I agree with you there, ma'am.'

'Then you are glad the wars are over?'

He was silent, debating whether to give her the answer that would do him the most good. But there was a stubborn streak in him that wouldn't allow it.

Finally, he said, 'I would be, except for my means of livelihood being gone now.'

'So that's all it meant to you! A job!'

'It was a job had to be done,' he said. 'Men like me, we saved the lives of a lot of soldiers. Kept them out of ambushes, among other things.'

'Men like you also led them into peaceful encampments,' she said. 'The Sand Creek massacre.'

'I wasn't at Sand Creek,' he said. 'I was only seven years old at the time.'

'I was speaking of your *kind*,' she said.

She was unfair, he thought. She had a mindset that he had no chance of changing. He would waste no more effort in trying. Let her keep her prejudices.

Wanting to clear up a point, he said, 'Are you just passing through here, ma'am?'

She gave him a wicked look. 'No, Mr Seaver. I was visiting the Western Shoshone reservation down on the Nevada line when I heard you were campaigning here for county law officer.'

'A long stage ride,' he said. 'For what purpose?'

'I'm sure you can guess. To put it bluntly, Mr Seaver, I have an interest in seeing that a man of your reputation does not get into office. I have a well-founded fear that any Indians unfortunate enough to be suspected of depredations against white ranchers or mining interests in your jurisdiction would be brutalized.'

11

'That's not so,' he said.

'I would not expect you to admit it.'

He fought down his anger.

She continued, 'Occasionally we have Indians slip off the reservations. Sometimes to hunt, when their government rations are not forthcoming. Sometimes they get into mischief. And that, precisely, is my concern—that even minor mischief could bring down heavy action on them by you and those who would be acting under your orders.'

He started to protest, but she held up a white-gloved hand.

'A matter of conditioning,' she said. 'Born of your years of warring against them.'

'I see you have a closed mind against me.'

'In this particular situation, yes, I have. I have strong sentiments against the mistreatment I've seen against the red race. So strong that I will fight against anything I believe could contribute to their receiving more of it.'

'A narrow viewpoint, ma'am.' Seaver stood up, staring down at her matching glance. 'You are a beautiful woman. I'm sorry your sentiments have turned you against me.'

He turned and walked out of the lobby, leaving her frowning after him.

*   *   *

'Well?' Warden said as Seaver entered the

office.

Seaver shrugged. 'A woman of strong prejudices,' he said.

'She's out to get you, then?'

'It appears so.'

'Damn! We didn't need that.'

'How do people get these damn-fool ideas?'

'They gather the ideas that reinforce their causes, Jon.'

'That's not fair.'

'Her type put themselves, body and soul, behind a cause they come to believe in,' Warden said. 'From there it's only a short jump to unfairness.' He paused. 'In a way, I myself believe there is much truth in her charges that the red man has been unjustly treated by the government.'

'Hell, I won't argue that. I've seen some of it firsthand. What I don't see is why she'd hold me responsible.'

'You've become a figurehead of a policy she hates, that's why. It has blinded her to particulars.'

'You can say that again.'

Warden was silent, then said, 'What do you intend to do about it?'

'Fight her, every step of the way.'

'How?'

'Speech for speech, if that's the way she wants it.'

'She's a better speaker than you are.'

'I don't doubt that,' Seaver said. 'But it's my

reckoning there's more sentiment on my side than on hers.'

Warden hesitated. 'Let's hope so, Jon. But I'm more in touch with townsfolks than you are. And I can tell you that times are changing, now that the Indian threat has lessened. And that massacre of the Sioux at Wounded Knee a year and a half ago had a lot to do with it.'

'I know,' Seaver said. 'I was there, remember.'

Warden frowned. 'God help us if Gordon finds that out!'

'She already knows. Made a point of telling me about it.'

'How did she know?'

'Took the pains to learn the army units involved, I suppose, and somebody searching the records for her discovered my name on the roster.'

'Then that's what turned her against you! When she heard you were running for office—'

'Exactly,' Seaver said. 'I tried to explain that there was wild shooting on both sides. Bullets flying everywhere. A lot of the killing shouldn't have happened. I admitted that.'

Warden shook his head in irritation. 'Listen to me, Jon. You're running for what amounts to a political office, more or less. And to be a politician, you've got to temper the truth with a little lying.'

'She's not a woman you can easily lie to,' Seaver said.

14

At two o'clock, Seaver was in front of the town hall, ready to speak. Warden stood beside him, about to give a few introductory words. They both stared at the gathered crowd of miners and townsmen.

'Figured to draw more,' Seaver said.

'It's that woman,' Warden said. 'She spread the word she'd be giving an impromptu talk outside the schoolhouse. There were women gathering there at least a half hour ago.'

'Like I said, Ray, women can't vote.'

'And like I said, she draws men too. Ones that would have been here otherwise.'

'She's got the looks to do that,' Seaver said.

'Nothing fair when a woman fights,' Warden said. 'They've got a code of their own.'

'Can't blame her for looks,' Seaver said. 'Well, get on with what you're going to say. This crowd isn't getting any bigger.'

Warden stepped to the portable podium he'd set up.

'Citizens of Silver City,' he said, 'I present to you your candidate for sheriff of Owyhee County. A man with singular qualifications for the job. A fighting man of courage, and a hero of the Indian wars. A man who served the army well with his well-honed skills at tracking down predators who raided towns of peaceful settlers such as yourselves. A man whose years of service helped immensely in bringing enemy

15

attacks to an end.

'A man who now offers those same unique skills to protect you from outlaw and criminal elements that have become the present enemy of our society.

'Men, I give you a man you have all heard of, a true man of the West. I give you Jon Seaver!'

There was moderate applause.

Seaver replaced Warden at the podium.

He looked out at the somewhat disappointing audience. There wasn't a woman among them, he noted. The reason was clear enough. The women were over at the schoolhouse, listening to that damned woman.

He felt his anger rising and tried hard to fight it down. He wanted to lash out at Ella Gordon, but his code of not disparaging women barred his doing so.

He forced himself to start out easily enough.

'Friends, I have resided among you these past several weeks. On many occasions I have made campaign speeches, setting forth what I believe to be the reasons you should vote for me in next week's election.

'My friend Ray Warden here has just reminded you of them once again. The showdown is near. I hope you have given my qualifications serious consideration. I want to be your sheriff, and I know I can serve you well.'

He paused, looking out at them and seeing something less than the approval he had

16

thought he'd seen the last time he addressed them.

Good God! he thought. Has that woman already destroyed my chances just by her presence in the town?

Not possible, he thought.

But at that moment he felt the need to put forth a defense, and he said, 'There are interests in this town, recently arrived, who are criticizing my reputation, because of their mistaken idea of what I did during my Indian-fighting days. I hope you don't let this criticism influence your vote.'

Some townsman at the front of the crowd called out, 'We've heard some of that criticism. And what answer do you have for it?'

For a moment Seaver was silent, but when his answer came, it was wrenched from his gut.

'Now that the Indian wars are over, and the settlers aren't scared for their lives any more, certain people meet me and ask how many peaceful Indians I killed during the fighting.

'I never killed none of them intentional,' he said.

CHAPTER TWO

Standing behind him and a little to one side, Warden muttered under his breath. When Seaver heard him, he immediately realized he'd

17

blundered. Now the very point of that woman's attack had been driven by himself into the minds of his listeners.

Warden was right. As a speaker, he was not the sharpest. He was a man of action, not of words. No match for Ella Gordon, that was sure.

He tried to think of a way to remedy his mistake, even as the townsman questioner pressed his point.

'Intentional or not,' the townsman said, 'such deeds were done, am I right?'

'Things happen in any battle where there are innocent people within range of fire between opposing forces,' Seaver said. 'Any such happenings that occurred, I regret. In some ways war combat is different from the kind of battle we're fighting against outlaws. Still, I maintain that my years of experience in the one can be tapped to be effective in the other. That's what I'm stressing—I will be an effective lawman. I will know how to run down outlaws on the dodge just as I knew how to track down Indian marauders. I will enforce the law because I have long lived under military discipline.'

The townsman spoke again. 'We already have a man in office who is serving us well. He has kept the peace in this town.'

Seaver, eyes on him, saw at that moment the brawny figure of Big Jim Halloran push forward through the crowd to stand beside his

18

spokesman.

Sheriff Halloran was an imposing figure of a man. Now middle-aged and graying, he still retained the physique of the lumberjack he once had been. He had a big voice too, and now it boomed out the big question, 'So why would these good folks want a change, Seaver?'

Why indeed? Seaver thought, and tried to answer the query. 'Sure, you've kept law and order here in Silver City, leastwise among the citizenry. But what about road agents holding up the stage and getting away? What about the bank robbery last month with a lone bandit riding off and eluding you?'

'This is a big county,' Halloran said. 'With a lot of space to disappear into.'

'I agree,' Seaver said. 'And that's just why a man tracker is needed. Somebody who can pursue an outlaw's trail and bring him in.' He paused. 'I am that man.'

'In this job,' Halloran said, 'it ain't that easy. You don't have the U.S. Army with you.'

'An army scout,' Seaver said, 'spends a lot of time far out in front of the troops. With only himself to depend on.'

'You're a fool to think you can beat me.'

'We'll see,' Seaver said.

'That we will,' Halloran said. 'Next week.' With that, he turned and walked away, his broad back giving the impression that he found Seaver not worth arguing with.

The bastard knew how to get under a man's

skin, Seaver thought angrily.

The townsman up front added fuel of his own by saying, 'Your kind maybe had their place once ... but your kind has seen their day.'

'We'll see,' Seaver said.

'Like Halloran says—' the townsman replied, 'next week.'

*   *   *

Next week came, along with a sizable celebration by Halloran of his victory.

Seaver was disappointed, of course.

But he had made a good showing. The balloting was close, with a spread of only a few hundred votes.

'You gave it a hell of a good go,' Warden said. 'You can take satisfaction from that. It proves a lot of folks still consider you a hero.' He paused. 'But that woman tipped the scales.'

'Maybe so,' Seaver said. 'But I won't fault her for her beliefs. Maybe I wasn't qualified. But a man whose means of livelihood is a thing of the past—he gets desperate enough to grab at chances.'

'I guess that's so,' Warden said. 'What plans do you have for the future?'

'None yet. During the campaign I wouldn't let myself think about losing. Foolish maybe, but that's the way I've always lived.'

'Well,' Warden said, 'it's been a pleasure working for you, and I'm sure you'll find something else. Will you be leaving soon?'

'Within a couple of days, I reckon. There's nothing left for me in this town.'

'Good luck in whatever you do.'

Seaver nodded.

Warden started to leave, then turned back to say, 'There was a time when you might have won, hands down.'

Seaver said nothing, and after a moment Warden left.

Yes, there was a time, Seaver thought. But in that time I didn't need it.

He remained secluded that night, sleeping on the cot in the office. Tomorrow I'll leave, he thought.

*   *   *

The sound of someone pounding on the door woke him in the morning.

It was Warden, whose first words came in a rush as Seaver let him in. Only one word caught his attention.

'Abducted?' Seaver said.

'Last night,' Warden said. 'I just got the particulars from a Halloran deputy.' Warden shook his head. 'Ella Gordon. Too damned bad it couldn't have happened a week or so ago, before she ruined your election bid.'

'Any suspects?'

'One. He was seen in the vicinity of the hotel. Where he had no reason to be.'

21

'Who?'

'It was an Indian off the Duck Valley reservation down on the Nevada border. Shoshone, name of Pandre. He was recognized by a freighter in town who hauls supplies there on occasion.'

'An Indian? By God!'

'Ironic, isn't it.'

'Couldn't be more so,' Seaver said. 'But why would an Indian do that?'

'Same reason a white man might.'

'Granted,' Seaver said, 'she is a mighty attractive woman.'

'I kind of figured you might take the news differently.'

'Then you don't know me. The abduction of white women is something I've encountered over the years. And I've seen the end atrocities of some. Not a pretty sight to see.'

'Yeah,' Warden said. 'I can believe that.'

'Halloran get up a posse?'

'Yeah. They rode off an hour ago, Halloran leading them himself.'

Seaver was silent. Then he said, 'I see he didn't ask me to join him. And he damn well knows that tracking Indians was part of my business.'

'Maybe he figured you wouldn't be interested,' Warden said. 'Her losing you the election.'

'I just told you how I feel about kidnappers of women.'

Warden nodded, but said, 'Halloran wouldn't have known that.' He studied Seaver's face. 'You still figuring on leaving town today?'

'No. Not now. I want to know how Halloran makes out. I just may wait and see.'

*   *   *

Three days later Halloran and his six-man posse returned.

Six range riders visiting from outlying cattle ranches, they had been the best men Halloran could muster on short notice in a town populated mostly by miners. Tough, hard men who had set out to run down one Indian, and his woman victim, and had failed.

Seaver happened to be on the street near the law office when they rode in. He saw at a glance that they had come back empty-handed.

Big Jim Halloran looked more beat than the rest of them. Big Jim was a town lawman, not much toughened by the saddle.

As he swung down heavily from his horse, his eyes caught Seaver's. Halloran held the stare speculatively for a moment before turning away.

Seaver was close enough to call, 'No luck, I see.'

Halloran looked at him again. 'Damn Injun headed for the mountains northeast. We lost his trail beyond the Snake River. He was in

Ada County by then. Out of my jurisdiction.'

'The sheriff there know what's going on?'

'I got a message off to him,' Halloran said testily. 'I know my business, Seaver.'

'I ain't arguing that anymore,' Seaver said.

The sheriff gave him a studying look. 'I guess the woman being took by that Injun makes you feel right pleased.'

'Well, it don't. I've seen what can happen to women taken like that.'

Halloran stood silent, thinking over his words.

The posse, having tied their mounts to a hitchrack, headed down the street toward a saloon.

Seaver said, 'What're you going to do about her now?'

'I'm going to work with any lawman has jurisdiction wherever she's taken. Ain't much more I can do just yet.'

'Goodbye, Ella Gordon,' Seaver said.

'Listen you, I'll be working on her case anyhow I can.' Halloran turned then and disappeared into his office.

Another day passed while the town buzzed with speculation about the kidnapping.

Then, on the second day, Halloran sent word to Seaver to come in for a discussion.

He was seated at his desk when Seaver arrived.

'Sit down, Jon,' the sheriff said.

So now it's *Jon*, Seaver thought. Be on

24

guard—Halloran the politician is going to work here.

Seaver stared at him in silence.

'I called you in to bring you up to date on the kidnapping,' Halloran said.

Seaver waited.

'I've been in touch with the Duck Valley Reservation, Jon. And what I've learned is this: That Shoshone Injun that stole Ella was an admirer. Two reasons, it seems. One, he was part educated and a rabble-rouser among his kind for better Injun treatment. And I guess the couple of times she visited the reservation down there, she kind of took him under her wing.

'And from that, according to what some of them other Injuns have said, the sonofabitch sort of got a case on her. Talked a lot about her. Like he'd like to have her as his squaw, and such.

'So he up and took her. And that's the way the situation stands.'

'I half-guessed that much,' Seaver said. 'You hear anything from Ada County?'

'Sheriff over there tracked him to Alturas County and lost the trail. I just got the wire.'

Seaver was silent for a long moment. Then he said, 'It looks like he might be headed for what they call the Primitive Area. If he gets into that, he may never be found.' He paused. 'Two thousand square miles of towering peaks, deep gorges cut by raging rivers, forests of

25

pine, spruce, and fir, and plenty of game he could live on. Deer, elk, mountain sheep in the high reaches.'

'You've been there?'

'On the south edge of it,' Seaver said. 'A long time ago. The rest I only know by hearsay.'

'Would you go in?'

'After the Indian and the woman?'

'What else?'

Seaver was silent with thought.

Halloran said, 'So now you're thinking how she helped to lose you the election.' He paused. 'Think about them other women taken by Injuns, like you said you seen.'

'What I'm thinking,' Seaver said, 'is that I'm tapped out moneywise. I'd need a grubstake. A horse. Provisions.'

'That bad off, eh? I'll deputize you, and the county will stand good for it.'

Seaver was silent again.

Halloran said, 'I'd go in after her myself, was I qualified. But you, if you ain't been living a lie all these years, this looks like a job you maybe done before.'

'I was about to say I'll do it,' Seaver said. 'Get me what I need, and I'll leave tomorrow morning. The further that Indian gets into that wild country, the harder he'll be to find.'

Halloran stood up and extended his hand.

Seaver shook it.

The sheriff grinned then and said, 'I been putting you to a test, Jon. Wanted to see if all

26

that hero rep of yours was bull, or if maybe some of it was true.'

Seaver did not smile. 'Hard to tell the fact from the fiction, I'll grant you that.'

'And now I'll tell you something else,' Halloran said. 'Been a reward posted already. By the Women's National Indian Association. That's the organization that sponsors Gordon. Five thousand dollars for her safe return.'

Seaver shrugged. 'And how much to bring in the Indian?'

'Hell,' Halloran said, 'they don't want him back. That'd only spoil the *good Injun* policy of theirs, if he had to stand trial.'

'I'll figure on leaving tomorrow then,' Seaver said.

*   *   *

He rode out of Silver City the next morning, on a horse and saddle provided by Halloran, with a sack of provisions tied behind the cantle.

Only the Colt .45 slung at his side, and the .44-40 Winchester carbine in its boot were his own.

Halloran was there to see him leave. 'Ride straight for Idaho City,' he said. 'Mining town northeast of Boise. Had a wire from the sheriff there. An Injun and a white woman was spotted yesterday by a placer miner as they camped on a creek. Miner thought they made a strange couple, but he didn't know about the

27

abduction till he come into town. Description seems to fit.'

'He seems to be making good time,' Seaver said. 'The Indian, I mean. Considering he's traveling with an unwilling companion.'

Halloran was silent.

His silence struck Seaver. 'That bother you?'

'Some, maybe.' Halloran said testily, 'Get on your way. That Injun's got a big lead on you.'

Seaver gave him a mock salute, and rode away.

*   *   *

It took him two and a half days of hard riding to get to Idaho City. He was thankful that Halloran had picked a strong bay gelding that had stamina to spare. He'd damn well need all of it if he was going to overtake the Indian and his captive.

CHAPTER THREE

Physically, it was the harshest experience she had ever had.

And now, exhausted by the fast-paced days the Indian had set, she sat on the ground, her aching back against a sloping boulder, and stared across the fire to where he stood

28

watching her.

He had stopped trying to converse with her. She spoke only when necessary, once her violent protest had failed to stop him in Silver City.

She had been a fool to venture forth onto the darkened street that night. But she had tired of her room, and the lobby, and had thought to take the outdoor air. Perhaps a brief walk to the end of the block.

Now, days later, she had gone what seemed like a thousand chafing saddle miles, her thighs made raw by the leather.

It could have been worse, she thought. He could have forced her to hoist her skirts to straddle the mount he'd brought for her.

He had, in fact, until they had ridden many miles. He'd finally halted and ordered her to get down. He reached into a saddlebag and tossed her a pair of worn but clean Levi's.

'You wear,' he said, his first words since he'd cursed as she raked her fingernails across his face in her vain attempt to avoid abduction back there in Silver City.

He had hit her as he cursed, his fist smashing against her jaw.

She had not regained consciousness until they were outside of town. Hours later she was clinging to the saddlehorn of a led horse. She was terrified and in shock.

When he gave her the pants she went behind a high clump of sage to strip off her skirts. He had thrown her a shirt as well, and she had dressed in the clothes as he had ordered.

She came back, carrying her female garb.

'That better, Ella,' he said.

There was strong moonlight on the Snake River plain where she judged they had reached, and now she could see him clearly and could study the familiarity of his face.

He saw her angry stare.

She said, 'Pandre, why have you done this?'

'You don't know?'

'Of course I don't!'

'But you know for long time I want you.'

Yes, she knew. But it shocked her into silence to hear him say it.

'You get back on horse,' he said. 'You find pants better to ride than woman dress.'

She climbed back into the saddle, but clung to her old clothing. She said, 'I demand you take me back to Silver City!'

He rode close, reached down, and grasped the hanging lead rope tied to her mount.

'Did you hear me?' she said.

'Sure, I hear. But I don't listen.' He kicked his horse then, stretched out the lead rope, and tugged her mount into following.

'You can't do this, don't you understand?' she said. 'It was bad enough that you periodically jumped the reservation.'

'That been me. So now I jump again.' He turned toward her and smiled, showing white teeth.

He was a handsome young Indian, she thought. In his mid-twenties. For some reason that raised her anger even more when she spoke again.

'You are a troublemaker. For me and for those I try to convince to help your people. You make white sympathizers lose their sympathy. Can't you understand?'

'Maybe,' he said. He paused, then said, 'I make *you* lose it, too, Ella?'

'Stop calling me Ella! My name is Miss Gordon.'

'Sure,' he said. 'Ella Gordon.'

'You have some education,' she said. 'You know better than to do the things you do.'

'Four year in missionary school,' he said. 'They try teach me be good Indian and have good life. But it don't been that way. You know that.'

'I've heard that complaint a thousand times,' she said.

'Because it true.'

She was silent; argument with him would do her no good.

'Where are you taking me?' she said.

'You see.'

'Where?' she demanded.

He did not answer.

I have met many Indians, she thought. Surely, I can find a way to cope with him.

Fighting him is not the way.

31

Now, days later, she had not yet figured out how. As she grew increasingly exhausted she feared she was further from finding the way with each passing mile.

They had skirted a few mining camps, where she had hoped she might escape to. Especially the first one, close to the trail he was taking. She had heard of Idaho City, and believed they were near it. But he swung wide so that she saw its crude buildings only from a distance.

There were others she glimpsed later, miles apart. And then there were none.

Now they were approaching a range of mountains and a wilderness area that was formidable to her.

She had traveled in the West, by train and stagecoach, but never through country like this. She was an Eastern woman, born and bred. And she had scant horseback-riding experience, only during brief interludes as a guest here or there of prominent ranch families who desired to host a writing and lecturing celebrity, though some were indifferent to her cause. Hosts who wanted to boast of her visit, to their elite friends in San Francisco.

Well, she was a long way now from such hosts. And she stared again across the fire at her present one.

She had not intended to speak. But the words came out anyway. 'I am hungry.'

He went over to one of his saddlebags and withdrew a strip of dried meat. He came around to her side of the fire and tossed it to her.

She was not adept at catching things, and it fell to the ground.

'I am not a dog, to be thrown food,' she said.

He met her eyes for a long moment. Then he moved to where the meat lay, picked it up, and held it gently toward her. 'Sorry,' he said.

She took it, angry at herself for doing so. She shook a bit of forest debris from it, and bit into it.

'We've been living on jerky for three days,' she said, chewing.

'Tomorrow, you eat better. Tomorrow, I hunt. Much good game in mountains ahead.'

'Why are you taking me there?'

'I told you before,' he said. 'I want you for my woman.'

She frowned.

He saw it and said, 'You don't like Indians?'

At that moment she could not bring herself to answer.

'Yes or no?'

'But this is different!' There was outrage in her voice.

'How is different?'

'Good lord, can't you see? This is a crime. Woman stealing! Don't you understand?'

'You don't want come?'

'Of course I don't!'

'I thought we be good friends, maybe,' he said.

'Never! Not this way!'

He appeared to be genuinely perplexed. 'I no understand.'

He had to be joking, she thought. Teasing, in that strange Indian way she had sometimes noticed among them. It had sometimes amused her. Now it turned her aghast.

'I do not want to be with you,' she said. 'Not this way.'

His face hardened. 'Too bad,' he said. 'This how it be.' He paused. 'You sleep now. Tomorrow maybe I shoot deer. You feel better then.'

'You fool!' she said.

'No fool. You see.'

'Never!'

Anger burned in her, igniting a sudden overpowering hate.

She was shocked by her feeling. Shocked even more as she heard herself saying, 'You stupid Indian!'

He stared down at her, silent, his black eyes hard. '*You* say that?'

Sudden shame struck her. 'I'm sorry.' She groped to explain. 'I didn't mean stupid because you are Indian. I meant stupid because of what you've done.'

'Same thing, I think. What I done, is because I been Indian. Indian want woman, he take. You don't know that, Ella?'

'That's not acceptable among your own people, and you know it!'

'Sure. Not to take woman of my tribe that way. But men of my tribe, they capture woman from other tribe is all right.' He paused, with a faint smile. 'You from other tribe, is true, no?'

'You have done wrong, and you know it.'

'Who say is wrong?'

'I say it!'

'You change mind.'

She was too exhausted to argue more. Her body cried for rest. She twisted from the rock she was leaning against and let herself stretch out. Fatigue closed her eyes.

Then she heard him move toward her and she was afraid he would attack her. She opened her eyes, about to cry out.

But he only leaned forward and spread a blanket over her, then turned away.

She slept.

*   *   *

Ella awoke at dawn, only partly rested, and went groggily through the preparations to move on.

Not until she was mounted and the agonizing friction of the saddle stung her to full wakefulness, did her thoughts go back to her words with Pandre the previous night.

Went back to them, and then beyond. Back to earlier brief encounters she'd had with him.

35

Suddenly she was struck by doubts of her own sincerity as an activist for his people.

Did she really understand them? Did she see them as individuals ... or only as a victimized group who had evoked her sympathy?

Reflecting now, she was struck by contacts with Pandre that might well have indicated his amorous interest toward her, had she ever even considered such a possibility. She remembered times when he might have been trying to signal such feelings, unrecognized by her because she never even saw him as a man.

There was a way he had awkwardly sought to get attention from her by boasting of some of his exploits as a youth, such as the time he ran away from the missionary school, ending his white-man education.

And more intimate conversations that she had passed off as his desire for friendliness and nothing more, as when he touched her lightly on the shoulder as they discussed her activist efforts.

Even that had not clued her in to his male yearnings.

From a white male it would have, she thought. But from an Indian, it hadn't.

Failing to win her affection any other way, he had turned to what he knew from his Indian culture: Capture the woman you wanted and get her to submit to you.

Specifically, where was it she had gone wrong with Pandre?

There was the time he had brought her a gift of a coat made from rabbit skins, sewn together by a female relative of his. It was tawdry by her standards, but she was courteous enough to ask if he personally had made it. He had been offended.

'I do not sew,' he'd said. 'Women sew. But I hunt to get skins. Hunting is man's work.'

She should have known that, of course.

'I do it for you,' he had added, watching her face closely.

She felt his steady gaze and gave him a polite smile, wondering how to refuse the gift.

'But I have a warm coat,' she said, touching the fox fur jacket she wore, purchased in San Francisco.

'You no understand,' he said. 'This mean something, me to you. I want that you have.'

'All right,' she said. 'Thank you.'

'You put it on,' she said. 'Wear now in front of my people here on reservation. They understand this mean something.'

'I'll put it away now,' she said. 'To wear later—when the weather is warmer. Your people know we are friends. They know I am a friend of all of you.'

'That not the same thing,' he said. 'You no understand.'

His insistent manner annoyed her. It was true that his people often had little to wear except skimpy clothes made from small-game skins.

But she did not feel she had to dress in like discomfort to show her concern for their welfare. Wasn't she devoting her life to trying to improve theirs? Shouldn't that be enough sacrifice on her part? Why couldn't he understand?

'I will put it away for now,' she said in a tone that ended discussion.

He had turned away in silence and strode off, leaving her uncomfortably mystified at his behavior.

And there was the time he had written her a scrawled note, during another of her reservation visits. At the time she had been impressed only in that it showed he retained some literacy from his sojourn in the mission school.

It was brief, a personal thank-you note for her efforts was the way she interpreted it. He had handed it to her as she passed by, and she could recall its wording now: *You are good friend for us Shoshone. And for me, you are more. Pandre.*

Since other members of the tribe frequently spoke their thanks to her, she had dismissed this as no more than his showing off his ability to write.

She remembered that she had stopped, scanned his note as he waited, then acknowledged it with a smile and a nod, and passed on, without so much as a backward glance.

It was strange that now, in her present predicament, she could recall such events, long forgotten.

Later, when he had begun his occasional troublesome forays to hunt and trespass on settlers' lands, she had become more aware of him; had, at one time, responded to a request by the Duck Valley Agent, Lawrence Miller, to come to the reservation to speak to Pandre.

Miller had written her:

This Indian teeters constantly on the verge of becoming a 'bronco.' He has sufficient ability to become a serious threat if he cannot be induced to mend his ways.

My own efforts in this regard have not been successful.

But he has bluntly professed to me his deep admiration for you. So, despite deep differences between you and me regarding administration of Indian Affairs, I would suggest that you might be one to influence him to mend his behavior.

She had been in Carson City when the agent's request reached her. And, as soon as her speaking engagements permitted, she had acceded to it.

It was unfortunate that when she finally arrived, Pandre was gone again.

The fortunate part was that, as almost always, he had gone alone.

To her knowledge, Indians were gregarious people, and when a 'bronco' jumped a reservation he often took at least a few followers with him, other like-minded braves.

Pandre was an anomaly in that he appeared to be a loner.

But, as Agent Miller's letter had gone on to say:

That could change any time. We've got other restive braves here. It wouldn't take much for Pandre to recruit a bunch if he so desired. As you probably know, in years past there were a number of marauding bands led by self-appointed leaders who kept eastern Nevada in a state of fear. At this late date, we don't want it to happen again.

She had left before Pandre returned to the reservation, and only now wondered if she could have influenced him as the agent had hoped.

And wondered if she had recognized his feelings toward her for what they were, and contended with them then, she could have prevented his present desperate action.

It bothered her most of all that she'd had a recent opportunity to do this, on her latest visit to Duck Valley. But stung by word that the Indian fighter, Seaver, was campaigning for office close by, she had foregone Pandre in her preoccupation with combating Seaver's endeavor.

CHAPTER FOUR

In the mining town of Idaho City, Seaver contacted the local sheriff, who had done little, it seemed, about the abduction beyond sending the wire to Halloran.

He did, however, direct Seaver to where the placer miner who had spotted the missing pair was working his claim.

Seaver wasted no time with the lawman and pushed on to find the gold seeker, a small, feisty oldster named Burton, busy with shovel and sluice box along a creek.

In answer to Seaver's questioning, Burton leaned on his shovel and said, 'Yeah, I seen the sonofabitch while I was here working. I was too busy at the time to give him and the lady more than a glance. Wish to hell I'd paid more attention, though. My camp, as you likely noticed, is back there in them cottonwoods. Wasn't until I quit here to make supper that I found he'd stole a sheepskin coat out of my tent.'

Seaver nodded. 'Nights will be getting cold up ahead where I think he's heading.'

'Hell, you ever see that Injun? He's a man near your size. And look at me—no way he could fit hisself into my coat.'

'Must have taken it for the woman,' Seaver said.

'Ain't like an Injun,' the miner said. 'I mean, to think of making a captive comfortable.'

'They may have been acquainted.'

Burton looked thoughtful. 'I thought so at the time. If she was unwilling, it seems like she would have hollered.'

'Did she see you?'

'I don't know. They was a ways back in the brush there. The Injun did for sure, looked over this way when he seen me working.' Burton gestured toward the east. 'You on their trail?'

'Yeah.'

'You look over there a hundred yards or so and you'll see their horse tracks heading northward.'

'Much obliged,' Seaver said. 'How many days since they went by?'

'Three, four days now.' The miner paused. 'Listen, you catch up with that red sonofabitch, try not to put a bullet through my sheepskin. And bring it back if you're coming this way.'

'I don't figure to puncture it,' Seaver said. 'Seeing, by what you say, it'd be the woman wearing it.'

'I was forgetting,' the miner said. 'Well, I wish you luck.'

'You figure I'll need it?'

'When you spend your life the way I do,' the gold seeker said, 'luck is what you live on.'

*   *   *

Four days later Seaver felt, rather than saw, he had entered the Primitive Area. There was an increased harshness to the lush terrain that seemed to have imperceptibly engulfed him.

And although he had once skirted the fringe of this rugged wilderness while tracking a band of renegade Nez Percé, he felt no familiarity with it now.

Too many years had passed, he thought. Too many years spent in other places.

But, although the region felt foreign, the tracks he'd followed from the mining camp had become familiar.

The Shoshone made no effort to hide them. Which indicated one of two things: he had a disdain for the local lawmen's tracking ability or, being primarily a reservation Indian, he had little knowledge of how to cover a trail.

Seaver was inclined to believe there was something of both involved here. And the fact was that even for a skilled lone warrior, it was seldom possible to hide trail sign completely, popular legend to the contrary. He had followed enough of them in his time to know this. With the woman riding beside her captor it would be foolish for the Indian to even try.

Seaver was gaining on them. He could tell by

the lesser dryness of the horse droppings.

He wondered if the Indian would even suspect a professional scout might be following him.

He doubted, too, that the woman would ever entertain the possibility. Certainly not that Seaver might be that scout. Not with the antagonistic feeling between them.

She wouldn't know about the reward posted by her sponsors, he thought. And that, of course, was what had brought him out here.

Or was it? He thought back to a few times in his career when he had gone out on a search, either with a detail or alone, for some rancher's wife missing after an Indian raid. Twice it had been for women taken from the scene of stagecoach attacks. Abductions of women were not uncommon in the West, both by Indians and by roving bands of outlaws. Twice he'd had a part in bringing back a rescued captive, although one woman had lost her mind from abusive treatment.

Such recollections stuck with a man, he thought, and could influence his later actions. Still, it was the reward that had triggered his decision, he told himself. He wouldn't be here if it wasn't for that.

He was sure of it.

*   *   *

They had eaten venison for several days now,

after Pandre had shot a couple of mule deer.

'My God!' Ella said. 'Is there nothing but meat? How long can we live on meat alone?'

'Long time,' he said. 'Maybe forever. In buffalo country, Indians used to live many months on only buffalo.'

'Well, I can't.'

'This no is buffalo.'

'I can't live on only meat.'

'Indian woman could.'

'I can't.'

'Now you know,' he said, 'how is with us.'

'I knew before.'

'No,' he said. 'You only think you know. Now you really know.'

'I can never be an Indian woman.'

'You can,' he said. 'I teach you how.'

'Are you crazy?' The words were wrenched from her.

'You think so?'

She almost blurted yes. But her years of defending his people restrained her.

'I find roots, berries, pine nuts,' he said. 'You not go hungry.'

'Don't you understand?' she said. 'Food is only part of it! Do you expect me to live in this wilderness?'

He did not answer at once, thinking.

She said, 'Did you hear me?'

'I hear,' he said then. 'Maybe I make mistake taking you for wife forever.'

'Now you're showing some sense!' She

45

paused, then said, 'Take me back to a town.'

He shook his head. 'I do, they hang my neck. I see one time they do to white man for steal cow. What you think they do to Shoshone who steal white woman?'

'I'll speak for you,' she said. 'I'll explain you made a mistake.'

'They don't listen to you. Not this time.'

She knew he was right.

In her anger she said, 'Oh, why did you do it?'

He stood up and came over to her and put his hand on her shoulder. He kneaded it with his strong fingers.

'This is why, Ella,' he said. 'Maybe not forever now, but for a while.'

She should have pulled away from him, she knew.

He sat down beside her and put his arm around her.

She did not move.

CHAPTER FIVE

Bart Dorsey and three of his wild bunch had left Salmon City three days earlier, after robbing the local bank of several thousand dollars.

Their intention had been to ride east into the Bitterroots, but Dorsey had changed his plan

46

when he caught sight of Chris Carter on the street and recalled the old Montanan was a onetime lawman with an extensive knowledge of that particular mountain range.

Dorsey led his men west instead, striking out for the Idaho Primitive Area, which they entered a day later, quickly shaking off a posse as they did so. Unfortunately, it was a place he had never been before.

Now, deep in the Area, he and his band were roaming aimlessly in the wilderness.

It was too late to try to back out now, he was sure.

He had it in mind to stay on a westerly course, figuring that eventually they'd come out on the other side. But he had overestimated his and his men's competence as woodsmen and underestimated the wildness of the region's topography.

And he did not know that Chris Carter was a tenacious member of the posse.

* * *

Chris Carter had joined the sheriff's posse as soon as the bank robbery was discovered. Sheriff Cram was thirty years younger than Carter's sixty and inclined to look upon him as being over the hill, despite his earlier stints as a town marshal, Bitterroot mountain guide, and occasional bounty hunter.

After a day of hard riding, the sheriff

announced they were giving up the chase instead of following the robbers into the wilderness. Hearing the oldster's protest, Cram frowned.

'I've been in there,' Carter said. 'Roughest country you ever saw, but nothing we can't handle.'

Cram was smart enough not to argue directly. Instead, he eyed the other men of the posse, saw their fatigue, read the reluctance in their faces.

'When was you in there, Chris?' he said.

'I was a guide for a army detachment went in during the Sheepeater Injun War in seventy-nine.'

'Been some years since then, Chris.'

'I don't forget too easy where I been.'

'We're turning back,' Cram said.

Carter's expression showed his disgust. He said, 'There's a bounty on Dorsey, ain't there?'

'I got a dodger in my pocket says that's so. A thousand dollars dead or alive. Nothing on the men with him, that I recall. 'Course, we ain't sure who they are.'

'Well, then,' Carter said, 'that's big money, from where I sit the saddle.'

Sheriff Cram said, 'Let's see how these other men feel about it.' He turned toward them. 'Any of you want to go into that wild area, risking ambush and God only knows what else, on the outside chance of finding Dorsey's bunch?'

Some of the posse looked a little sheepish, not meeting Chris Carter's eyes as he stared at them, but none gave an affirmative answer.

'There's the vote, Chris. We're turning back,' Cram said. 'There's eight of us in this party. A thousand dollars split eight ways ain't worth going into that country, my way of thinking.'

Carter's mood had a sudden change. 'I see your point,' he said. 'But split only one way, now that's a sizable sum.'

Cram gave him a long stare. His irritation left him, replaced by a look of grudging respect.

He said, 'You'd go in there alone after them, Chris?'

'Ain't often a man my age gets a chance at that kind of money any more, Sheriff. With a little luck I just might bring Dorsey out and deliver him to you and claim that bounty.'

'Well, old man,' Cram said, 'if you can do that, you'll need this to identify him.' He reached into his pocket, withdrew the dodger with Dorsey's photo on it, and handed it to Carter.

*   *   *

Bart Dorsey rode in the lead of his three men, his face hiding his concern, a trick he'd learned long ago as an army officer. Always look competent, he thought. Don't let your troops know you're lost in this maze of canyons, creeks, gorges, and timbered slopes.

Now, riding their tired mounts up a sharp, pine-covered rise, they came upon a scene that brought them to a startled halt.

Below them, down in a ravine encampment near tethered horses, an Indian and a white woman were sitting side by side, with the Indian embracing her.

'By God!' Dorsey said. 'Look at that!'

'Don't make no noise,' one of his men, Sandow, said. 'Let's just watch this.'

But one of the others, Bunce, said, 'That's a lady-looking woman down there, Bart. Wasn't there something in a newspaper headline back there in Salmon about a Injun running off with one like her?'

'I didn't see any,' Dorsey said. 'I was too busy planning the robbery details.'

'Well, I seen it. Hell there was a copy of it on display outside a print shop as we rode in.'

'Indian ran off with her? Give a reason?'

'I only seen the headline, dammit! But you can see the reason right there in front of your eyes,' Bunce said.

'And a damn good reason,' Sandow said.

'Let's get down there and break it up before he has his way with her,' the third man, Griffin, said. 'I'd hate to see a Injun do that.'

'Let them alone. I want to watch,' Sandow said.

'Dorsey?'

'We'll break it up,' Dorsey said.

'Hell!' Sandow said. 'Why?'

'Because that's the way I feel about it,' Dorsey said. 'Ride in with your guns drawn.'

'Suppose he uses her for a shield?'

'Suppose he does. Do you see he has any weapon handy?'

Sandow laughed, but none of them answered.

They spread out a few feet apart and rode down the slope.

*　　*　　*

It was Ella who saw them approach.

She reacted with a violent shove, breaking loose of Pandre's embrace.

Startled, he reached out to her.

She said, 'On the slope!'

He twisted to see, starting to rise to move toward his weapons lying yards away.

'Hold it!' Bart Dorsey called. 'Hold it, right there!'

*　　*　　*

It was several hours later that Seaver came upon the now empty scene. A few minutes' search revealed signs of what had happened, and he silently cursed his luck.

Who were the riders, and what did they want with the Shoshone and the woman?

51

In his mind he tried to picture the answer, and he did not like what he saw. Any riders in this wilderness were likely to be renegades of one sort or another. And renegades meant trouble for the woman.

The tracks of his quarry had now nearly reversed into a northwesterly direction, accompanied now by those of the new riders, who he discovered had arrived from the east.

Was it possible the Shoshone had been impressed as an unwilling guide and that he was deliberately leading them north of his own trail into the area, hoping to lose them?

They must be poor trackers themselves, he thought. But this was not too unusual. It had been Seaver's experience that, like Sheriff Halloran, most men were not good at reading trail sign.

He now set about following the new tracks that diverged considerably. In this rough terrain the Indian would find it easy to fool inexpert woodsmen.

The Shoshone might have done a stupid thing in abducting the woman, but in his own way, he was sharp enough. But how long could the Shoshone fool his captors? Sooner or later some one of them would wise up, bringing unpredictable consequences.

And now Seaver found himself with a strangely heavy worry about the woman's fate at the hands of these new captors. He shoved it irritably from his mind. At least she was still alive.

But the worry kept returning. Something in his code toward women, he supposed, kept driving it back and giving an urgency to his effort to overtake them. And when he caught up with them, spotting in the timber their temporary encampment, the urgency reached its peak.

Directly in front of where he had crept, after tying his horse a distance away, he saw her.

She was alone, possibly on her way back from a relief break.

A moment later, though, she was confronted by a slim, black-bearded man in range clothes. Startled, she shrank back and turned to get away from him. He grabbed her in his arms, drawing her hard against himself, grinning. A moment later he had thrown her to the ground and dropped in a sprawl on top of her.

Seaver came out of his crouch and started forward, but at that moment the Shoshone appeared with a chunk of firewood in his hand, which he brought down on the attacker's head.

Seaver halted, staying hid.

The Shoshone grabbed the attacker and dragged him off her. He then jerked the man's revolver from his holster and held it against his head.

Ella Gordon cried, 'Pandre, no!'

The Shoshone looked at her and said, 'But you my woman, Ella. I kill for you.'

'No!' she said. 'They'll kill you if you do!'

Seaver was close enough to hear their words and was struck by them. It wasn't what he would have expected to hear between captor and captive, he thought.

As the Shoshone hesitated, another man arrived on the scene. He had a gun drawn and aimed at the Indian.

'Drop it, Indian!' he said.

There was a moment of uncertainty, and Seaver found his own gun in hand.

Then the Shoshone obeyed the order.

Ella spoke. 'He was only protecting me!'

The man nodded. 'I can believe that,' he said. 'Sandow isn't one to trust around women. That's why I came looking when I found him missing.' He picked up Sandow's gun and stuck it in his belt.

Sandow was beginning to stir, muttering incoherently, then opened his eyes and looked up. 'Dorsey, this damn Injun clubbed me!'

'I'd have done it myself, if he hadn't,' Dorsey said. 'You know my orders about the woman.'

Sandow got to his feet, holding his hand against the back of his head. 'Hell, them orders ain't reasonable, not with a looker like this wench. A man can't control hisself, if he's halfway normal.'

'Get back into camp,' Dorsey said.

'Give me my gun so's I can shoot this redskin sonofabitch!'

'You fool, he's the one going to guide us out of this maze of a wilderness.'

54

'You don't know that,' Sandow said.

'I'm betting on it.' Dorsey gave the Indian a hard look. 'If he doesn't, I'll take a gun to him myself.'

Sandow grudgingly turned toward the camp, grumbling, 'Hell of a way to treat a man only acting natural.'

Dorsey turned to Ella. 'I'm sorry, ma'am. I have given all of them orders not to touch you.'

She nodded, not looking at him until she felt his glance holding on her. She faced him then, met his eyes, and was surprised at what she saw.

There was male desire there, too. But there was also respect.

Dorsey said to her, 'You and the Indian follow Sandow.'

They moved then in single file back toward the camp, Dorsey keeping an eye on all of them.

CHAPTER SIX

They broke camp while Seaver watched, glad he'd left his mount at a distance that would not betray his presence.

As he had judged from their tracks, there were the four strangers holding his own quarries. Hardcases all, he was certain, having now heard two of them address each other by

55

name. He recalled there had been a wanted poster about a Dorsey on the wall of Sheriff Halloran's office.

Seaver had scanned it only briefly, and now cursed himself for not noting what reward had been posted.

Strange, he thought, how such information had taken on an importance to him, now that he was no longer on a steady army payroll. All these years, money had been only a minor concern.

Now on his own for the first extended period since his adolescence, he realized its importance for survival.

He had sometimes wondered at the re-enlistments of non-officers in the army. They had a miserable life, for the most part.

Now he knew the answer. For most of them, it was perhaps the only way they knew to survive. At least until death did them part, he added ruefully. He had seen plenty of them die.

For the rest of that day and the next, he followed Dorsey's bunch and its captives, using his skills honed over the years to avoid detection.

Progress was slow in the rugged terrain. There seemed to be no trails, or if there were, Pandre was deliberately staying clear of them.

He would likely know, Seaver thought, that once the bunch got free of the Primitive Area, his usefulness would terminate. And probably his life as well. It might be a no-win situation

56

for the Shoshone, because Dorsey's patience could be wearing thin.

And what then would happen to the woman?

The wonder goaded him. The Indian had saved her from rape once. What would happen if he was killed?

Seaver had to take action. But at the moment the only action open was one that did not set well with him. Sniping in cold blood had always gone against his grain, even during the war years. But in war you did what you had to do. And this was a war. Albeit a private one, a mercenary one.

The odds against him were heavier now. He had to do what had to be done.

Except that he couldn't bring himself to do it. It wasn't really a war, was the thought that kept coming up to stop him. It was a private conflict for personal gain. That made the difference.

That made it murder.

But how else to singlehandedly take the woman from the hardcases?

With the Shoshone an unknown quantity in any action.

*   *   *

Ella kept wondering if there was some way she could use Dorsey.

There was that deference in his attitude

toward her, and the fact that he spoke like an educated man.

He presented an imposing figure, she thought. In his late thirties perhaps, lean and hard, with a weathered face that held a trace of distinction.

Mounted, he looked like a range rider, but afoot he carried himself in a way that hinted of the military. As did the way he spoke. Sternly to the men, courteous to her.

All of this aroused her curiosity about his background and how she might use it to her advantage.

She had thanked him, of course, for coming to her rescue from Sandow's attack.

'Something I would do for any woman,' he said. 'I do not tolerate the crime of rape, ma'am.' He paused. 'Beyond that, I do not tolerate disobeying of my orders. I had given the command that you were not to be molested.'

'Apparently your command is not always obeyed,' she said.

'These are not soldiers, ma'am. They are men accustomed to flaunting authority.'

She'd already gotten that impression, but did not say so. 'Might I ask, Mr Dorsey, why you have taken my Indian companion and myself as captives?'

He hesitated, then said, 'Why, I believe he too had dishonorable intentions toward you.'

A faint flush came over her face.

'And one of my men recalled seeing a news item that a white woman had been abducted by one of his kind.' He was studying her closely as he spoke. 'I have asked you before, ma'am, if you are that woman. And you have not answered. I am still waiting to find out.'

She was silent.

'I would appreciate an answer,' he said.

'Yes and no,' she said finally.

'Yes and no, ma'am?'

'The Indian has not harmed me. As a matter of fact, he has professed infatuation.'

Dorsey gave the faintest of smiles. 'I can understand that, ma'am. So that's the story?'

'Not all. Mr Dorsey, did you read the news item you mentioned?'

'No. My men saw only a news headline.'

'I am Ella Gordon,' she said.

The name seemed not to register on him.

'An activist for Indian rights,' she said.

His expression changed. 'That Ella Gordon! Of course! I have heard of you, ma'am.'

'So I hesitate to make a charge against my companion. Can you understand that, sir?'

'I have come to believe people may do almost anything, Miss Gordon.'

'Indeed? And what are your intentions toward us?'

'I intend to use the Indian to guide us out of this blasted wilderness,' he said. 'And I could not leave you here alone.'

'That's all, Mr Dorsey?'

'Not quite, I'm afraid. There may be a reward for your return. That, too, is of interest to me.'

'I overheard your men discussing a bank robbery,' she said. 'Is that your profession, Mr Dorsey?'

'You are blunt with your questions, ma'am.'

'So you don't deny it?'

'You heard the men talking,' he said.

*　　　*　　　*

Seaver was still watching. Following the group, but waiting, using his experience to keep hidden while scrutinizing them for a chance to take action.

Bank robbers the captors of Gordon might be, but apart from Sandow's foiled attempt on her, she seemed in no imminent danger.

And he was not a lawman concerned with their banditry, he told himself.

But the bay gelding Sheriff Halloran had picked for him brought about an accident that caused a break in his routine. And his thinking. Seaver had tethered his horse at the site of his cold camp, a couple of miles from those he followed.

He awoke at first light to find that the horse had broken loose during the night and the hoofprints led in the direction of his quarry.

Seaver cursed the animal, all the time feeling his curses should be directed at himself for his negligence in securing the animal.

It wasn't unusual for a horse, breaking free, to seek the company of other horses. And if this had happened, he could be in trouble, he thought.

A moment later, Dorsey and two of his henchmen stepped out of the surrounding growth, their weapons drawn.

One of them was Ella's recent attacker.

Dorsey said, 'Sandow, take his gun.'

'He don't have no badge,' Sandow said. 'Maybe a goddamn bounty hunter.'

'Take his gun, I said.'

'Sure,' Sandow said. 'Just you keep your own pointing at him.'

Seaver was holding his hands high. He figured this was no time for heroics.

Dorsey said, 'Your horse paid us a visit during the night. It wasn't hard to backtrail him.'

'I figured,' Seaver said. 'I was about to take to his trail myself.'

'That a fact?'

'I'm not fond of walking.'

'What're you doing here?'

'Passing through.'

'Well, I can see that,' Dorsey said. 'But it's the reason you're passing through this wilderness I'm interested in.'

Seaver was silent.

Sandow said, 'I can make him talk.'

'Time for that later,' Dorsey said. 'I want to

get back to camp. I don't trust what the Indian may be up to, with only Griffin guarding him.'

He addressed Seaver again. 'You were about to trail your horse. You can do that now. Start walking.'

'What about my saddle and bedroll?' Seaver said, gesturing to where they lay on the ground.

'Our horses are back there in the timber. You can toss your bedroll behind a cantle. You can shoulder your saddle and grubsack.' Dorsey turned to his other man. 'Bunce, you give him a hand with that gear.'

Bunce complied.

They started off, Seaver walking heavily with his load.

As they drew close to the camp, he saw Ella look up at them with a surprised stare. The Shoshone was sitting on the ground, the hardcase Griffin nearby with a rifle in his hands.

The Shoshone watched them without expression.

But when Seaver, ahead of the riders, drew near, Ella said, 'You!'

He wished she had remained silent.

'You know each other?' Dorsey said.

She could not deny it now.

'What is his name, Miss Gordon?'

She hesitated.

'Miss Gordon?'

'Seaver,' she said. 'Jon Seaver.'

Dorsey looked startled. He turned toward

Seaver.

'That right?'

Seaver nodded.

'The famous army scout?' Dorsey said. 'I recall the name.'

'Have we met?' Seaver said. 'Before this, I mean.'

'I only know of you by hearsay.'

'But you have been army yourself?'

'A fact hard to hide, I guess,' Dorsey said.

Seaver had his own sudden recollection. '*Captain* Dorsey, wasn't it? Cashiered out of the service, the way I heard it.'

Dorsey shrugged.

'For embezzlement,' Seaver said.

'Money has always been my weakness, Seaver.'

'And now robbing banks.'

'My weakness, like I said.'

'What do you want with the woman?'

'My guess is she is not a wholly willing companion to the Indian. If so, there could be a reward out for her return.'

'Money again?'

'Exactly,' Dorsey said. 'And what's your interest?'

Ella had been listening. Her interest sharpened, and she said to Seaver, 'A reward?'

He said, 'That's what brought me into this wilderness, ma'am.'

'May I ask who posted the reward, Mr Seaver?'

'That Indian-loving organization you speak for.'

'Must you be so crude in your speech, Mr Seaver?'

'I've led a crude life, ma'am.'

Dorsey said, 'So there is a reward!' He paused, then said, 'Seaver, you and I can do business together.'

Seaver studied him coolly. He said nothing.

'Can you find us a trail out of this damn jungle?'

'Isn't the Indian doing it?'

'He's supposed to.'

'Why?'

'For the same reason I'll offer you. A guarantee of the woman's safety.'

Seaver still studied him. He said, 'Yesterday, your guarantee came close to being worthless.' He gestured toward Sandow, standing behind Dorsey.

'You saw that?'

'The Indian saved her.'

'I've got one man who's hard to control,' Dorsey said.

'So I noticed.'

'If he makes another move like that, I'll shoot him.' Dorsey turned, gave Sandow a hard stare.

'You should have done it yesterday,' Seaver said.

'He's a good man in our business,' Dorsey said. 'If he tries that again, though, the fact

64

won't carry weight.'

Bunce and Griffin were standing by, and they both nodded.

'And after we're out?'

'We can make another agreement on splitting the reward.'

'And if I don't agree?'

'You're forgetting we have the woman now. We could claim the whole reward.'

'You might find it hard to collect. Do you know you're on a wanted dodger?'

'Sandow isn't. He's new to us.'

'You couldn't trust him with her, and you know it,' Seaver said.

'I'll figure out a way. Or there could be a gentlemen's agreement between us.'

'You still think of yourself as an officer and a gentleman?' Seaver said.

'An officer, no.'

'But still a gentleman? Hard to believe.'

'I would abide by an agreement between us,' Dorsey said.

'We'll talk about it later,' Seaver said.

'You'll lead us out of here, then?'

Seaver shrugged. 'Why not? We're going the same way.'

'The Indian may try to trip you up.'

'I can handle the Indian,' Seaver said.

'Yeah. You've got that reputation, Seaver.'

'What do you mean by that?'

'Indian killer, isn't that where your renown comes from?'

'And yours? The recollection is coming back to me that your command annihilated an encampment of sleeping Indian families. And it so happened they were non-hostiles.'

'I was following a colonel's orders. And he, in turn, was acting on faulty military intelligence.'

Seaver was silent.

Dorsey said, 'Intelligence supplied him by a drunken scout with a private quarrel against an Indian chief.'

'There were good and bad scouts during the wars,' Seaver said.

'It shattered my morale,' Dorsey said. 'I drank to drown out the memory, but it did no good. I gambled, and I lost heavily. That didn't help either. All it did is run up debts.'

'Other men have done the same,' Seaver said.

Dorsey seemed not to hear him. His mind was directed inward. 'So I owed money to men who despised me. After murdering a village of friendly Indians, what did a crime of minor embezzlement mean to me? It was insignificant by comparison.'

Seaver was silent again.

'I was no longer any good as a combat officer,' Dorsey said. 'Still, foolishly, I was entrusted with company funds.' He paused. 'Well, you can guess the rest.' He paused again. 'And I've always had this lust for money.' Another pause. 'Remember that.'

66

I'll remember that, all right, Seaver thought. I'll remember when it comes time to collect that reward. It isn't something I'll be likely to forget.

*   *   *

Neither Seaver nor the Shoshone found other than game trails. Deer were plentiful, and twice they spotted elk.

So they had meat to eat, and Seaver had a directional sense that kept them working westward, even as the Indian had been doing. Pandre did not argue. He seldom spoke.

Seaver believed he was brooding over his thwarted abduction of Gordon and likely was biding his time, hoping for a chance to break away from his captors and take her with him once more.

The likelihood of that was small. The Indian was too closely watched by all the rest of them.

Including Ella? Yes, Seaver was certain of that now.

Whatever her feelings toward Pandre, he was sure she resented being kidnapped by him.

Although, he thought, the earlier intimacy of camping together night after night might have affected her emotions in ways unknown to him. As he had told himself before, he was not knowledgeable in the ways of women.

It was something that bothered him now for the first time, and he wondered why this should be.

He had talked to her, of course. But there were some things a man like himself simply did not ask outright of a woman, much as he would like to know. A man did not say to her, 'Tell me, ma'am, have you been sleeping with this Indian?'

She had been the one to ask questions. She had overheard part of the discussion he'd had with Dorsey.

'There is a reward out for my rescue, then?' she said.

'There is.'

'I should be flattered.'

'Are you?'

'Of course. Why wouldn't I be?'

'I don't know, ma'am. I'm not good at reading women.' He hesitated, then said, 'The Indian having taken you, like they told me in Silver City, it's hard for me to figure you'd be as friendly with him as you appear to be.'

'I knew him slightly from visiting the reservation.'

'So I heard,' Seaver said. 'But, even so.'

'He is of the people for whom I am committed to bettering their conditions, Mr Seaver.'

'Seems like you're willing to put up with a lot from their kind,' he said.

She gave him a sharp look, studying his eyes before she spoke. 'Yes, I suppose I am. That's because I've come to realize their behavior is

68

often the result of a very different culture.'

'Well, I know about that all right,' he said.

'Then you understand Pandre?'

'I understand him,' Seaver said. 'It's you, ma'am, I don't.'

*   *   *

Chris Carter watched from hiding. He had finally caught up with his quarry. He recognized Dorsey from the photo on the dodger.

But he now faced a complication.

Dorsey, and his three confederates, had with them three others, two of whom he recognized from photos in recent news stories: Ella Gordon's abduction and Jon Seaver's campaign for sheriff. The third, the Indian, he guessed might be her abductor.

One other thing he noted: Seaver wore an empty holster, which meant he was a captive. Carter weighed all this, then made his decision.

This was not the time to make his move.

CHAPTER SEVEN

Two days later Seaver became aware that their progress was being watched.

'Sheepeater Indians,' Seaver said.

Ella gave him a blank look, then glanced

questioningly at Pandre.

The Shoshone nodded. 'Maybe so,' he said.

Ella turned back to Seaver. 'Sheepeaters? Here and now?'

'Remnants of a band that fought the army back in seventy-nine,' Seaver said. 'Most of them gave up and were sent to the Fort Hall reservation. But there's been a rumor that a few kept living here. This seems to bear that out.'

'Is true, maybe,' Pandre said. 'I hear same thing from my own people sometimes.'

'Are they—?' Ella said. 'I mean—do they still dislike whites?'

'Are you worried?' Seaver asked.

'Of course I am!' She frowned. 'But they may have a reason to hate whites. It depends on the treatment they got from the army.'

'The army did its job,' Seaver said.

'As always,' she said.

'Exactly.' Seaver said. 'And let me tell you why.' He paused, then said, 'The story was the Sheepeaters had been formed from outlaws of the Shoshone and Bannock tribes who periodically sallied forth from the Salmon River Mountains to rob and murder ranchers and miners. They got their name from the heavy diet of mountain sheep they supposedly lived on. To my knowledge, their defeat by the army ended their raiding thirteen years ago. I'm telling you what I been told.' He paused, then admitted, 'I wasn't here at the time. I was down in Arizona against the Apaches.'

'So why are they watching us?' she said.

'It's natural enough. We're strangers passing through their territory. Curiosity is to be expected.'

'That's all, then?'

'Likely is,' Seaver said. 'Provided none of us provoke them.'

'Mr Dorsey should be told about this,' she said.

'Dorsey will be told,' he said. 'Immediately. We've got to rely on him to control his men. We don't want one of them to sight a redskin, spook, and fire a weapon at him.'

Dorsey had seen them in discussion, and now approached.

'What's the parley about?' he said. Suspicion showed on his face.

Seaver told him.

'How many are there?' Dorsey said.

'I don't know. I'm sure we're outnumbered, though. Warn your men to keep armed, but to make no aggressive moves.'

'Will do,' Dorsey said.

'Make it an *order*, Captain.'

Dorsey searched his face for any sign of sarcasm. Finding none, he gave a short nod and turned away to gather his men into a group and address them.

As Seaver watched he saw them begin to cast alarmed glances into the surrounding growth.

Hostile Indians were supposed to be a thing

71

of the past, Seaver thought cynically. He hoped that in this case it was true.

*   *   *

Now that the travelers were aware of their presence, the Indians began to show occasional quick glimpses of themselves.

And so long as the whites kept moving, they seemed to ask for nothing more.

Seaver spoke to Dorsey of this. 'They don't want trouble,' he said. 'They only want us out of their adopted territory.'

'Good enough,' Dorsey said. 'All I want is to get out of it.'

*   *   *

It was Sandow whom Ella feared the most. He continued to stare at her whenever she was within his sight.

It was a look she could not analyze for certain. At first she thought it was hate because of Dorsey's threat of violent punishment if Sandow ever again aggressed against her.

Then, later, when chance threw them closer together during periods of halt, she recognized the blatant lust in his eyes, as strong as it had been in those terrible moments of his attack.

What was wrong with the man, she thought? Even Pandre, telling her frankly of his desire, had shocked her less than did Sandow's stare.

The other men, warned off by Dorsey, took pains to keep their distance and their glances away from her.

So she had protection by the former officer. And by Seaver, she thought. And by Pandre.

But still she felt terror of Sandow.

Pandre, too, occupied much of her thought. Now, as a captive of the wild bunch, he seldom spoke. Even to her.

He had adopted an impassive facial expression that revealed nothing. He did occasionally converse with Seaver concerning the route they were seeking out of the wild area, but only if Seaver questioned him. Otherwise he remained in isolation among the rest.

They were an odd lot of fellow travelers through the wilderness, she thought. Although they had a common object during this journey, she sensed that there lay ahead some potentially explosive interactions once they were free of the area.

Once out, they would be individuals again, with conflicting aims, pitted against one another.

And where would she fit in these confrontations?

At that moment she had the feeling she might be nothing more than a pawn.

Another thought struck her then: she may have been unfair in voicing her opposition against Seaver in his bid for election in Silver

City. She had believed that Seaver was not the man to be placed in a position where he might be overly harsh on errant Indian offenders.

Was it a bias? she thought. She had never thought of herself as having biases before. Her emotions ran strong for what she believed, she had known that. But had they caused her to prejudge him, to overreact?

Self-doubt had never been a part of her character. Now, since her abduction, it tugged at her.

*   *   *

She knew of the Sheepeater Indians, of course.

Not from personal contact, but from reading. Despite her questioning of Seaver about the tribal remnant, she probably knew more of their background than he did.

She knew about the war back in '79, but her belief about its cause differed from his.

He had said the army was called in to pursue the Sheepeaters into their mountain hideouts after they robbed and killed ranchers and miners.

This, she thought, was just part of the old falsehoods so often used in other parts of the West. False accusations by whites had often sent the army into action, with one of two results. One got rid of Indians on land coveted by miners or ranchers. The other was advantageous to merchants with supplies to

74

sell to the military during a local campaign.

In the sixties gold had been discovered in the Boise Basin and on the Salmon River. At Leesburg, just west of Salmon City, seven thousand placer miners overran the Sheepeaters' important fishing villages in the mid-seventies.

Other locations of the Sheepeater terrain were likewise confiscated or destroyed by whites. Some Sheepeaters possibly fought back against this encroachment, Ella might admit, but she believed flatly that if they had, there was legitimate cause.

Even as she now believed that those watching her and her companions would wreak no harm, providing no provocation occurred.

*   *   *

Her thoughts were interrupted by the eerie feeling she was being watched. At this time they were riding in single file along a game trail through a stretch of pines.

She turned in her saddle, and found Sandow's stare drilling into her own. He held it unwaveringly.

Then he smiled.

And she shuddered.

*   *   *

Chris Carter had just missed blundering into the Sheepeaters as they took up their early surveilance of the whites.

He had been holding his distance on their north flank, and the Indians had come out of the southeast.

It was a case of who saw who first, and Chris had been the lucky one.

Not that the redskins seemed hostile. Curious, he thought, was more like it. Still, once you'd fought a tribe, you remained forever leery.

He was confident of being able to remain undiscovered, but his main concern was what action they might take if their curiosity about the whites changed to animosity. Although he had no count of their number, he had spied on their movements around their encampments enough to judge they could easily overwhelm the whites if they attacked.

The presence of the Sheepeaters complicated a bad situation.

CHAPTER EIGHT

The Indian band of about three dozen had been on their way to an area where they expected to find good elk hunting. Of this number, a dozen were hunter braves. The others were women and children, except for a couple of old men. For two days now, some of the braves had a group of whites under surveilance.

A sixteen-year-old Sheepeater girl, who considered herself a woman, was more curious than most. She had seen a white prospector or two in her life, and wanted to know more about those now being watched, especially after hearing the braves talk in the evening camps.

The women and children had been warned to stay close to the camp, where some of the men always remained to protect them.

Protect them from what? the young woman wondered.

She became bold enough to ask this question of Tamanmo, the young leader of the band. She had hopes of becoming Tamanmo's wife, and her question, too, was a way to open a conversation with him.

He had smiled at her brashness, but had given her a frank answer. 'The whites always bear watching when they are close.'

'They are enemies?'

'There is not a war between us,' he said. 'Not for many years. But they have tricked us in the past.'

'How do *you* know that?' she said. She let her eyes survey his young, lithe body.

'The old ones, who lived in those times, tell of it.'

'I see.'

In his mid-twenties, he was old enough to

sense her ripening interest in him, and was both amused and titillated by it. 'You are safe in the camp,' he said.

She turned away from him, her curiosity only increased by the little he had told her.

Thinking back, she recalled she had been a child when last she had seen a white. Now, knowing there were some not more than a couple of miles away was tantalizing to her.

*   *   *

Seaver had begun to suspect that the Sheepeaters' watch on him and the others was becoming more sporadic, ceasing each time the whites made camp. He assumed they returned to their own camp at such times.

Which meant the Indians were losing interest. And that was good.

It was always a strain to be under the eyes of strangers, hostile or not.

He had been particularly concerned whenever Ella withdrew into the brush for privy moments. She appeared fearful at such times, reluctantly driven by her needs.

At such times, if he noticed, he took pains to watch Sandow, whom he still did not trust to abide by Dorsey's orders or threats.

Twice, Seaver had noticed that Sandow disappeared for short periods, although never when Ella was out of sight.

Once, Seaver had directly questioned him,

mentioning that a lone white could be a likely temptation to any band of Indians who had once engaged in war against the army, however long ago.

'Just doing a little scouting on my own, Seaver,' Sandow said. 'I ain't so sure as you that they don't have hostile intent.'

'It's your neck,' Seaver said. 'And personally I wouldn't care if they took you. But if a bunch of Indians gets a taste of white blood, they just might get a quick taste for more. I've seen it happen.'

'I ain't about to let them take me,' Sandow said. 'I can take care of myself.'

'I've heard that refrain before,' Seaver said. 'Many times in a lot of places.'

'This time you can believe it,' Sandow said. 'Ain't nobody I trust to take care of me like I do my own self.'

*   *   *

The Sheepeater girl's curiosity grew.

She had always been of a venturesome nature. She decided to slip away for a clandestine look at the whites.

She knew, from overhearing the braves' talk, the direction to find the whites' gathering. It was easy enough to slip away from her own people, although she knew she might expect some censure when she returned.

The risk was worth it, she felt. Her

sometimes bold exploits had brought punishment in the past, but she had learned to live with it. It was the price she had to pay for satisfying her spirit.

She felt her blood race as she made her way through the timber and undergrowth. She approached cautiously, alerted by the scent of their campfire.

As the scent became stronger her excitement grew. Then she saw the white man.

A slim, black-bearded man, who seemed to be scouting for something.

And at that moment he saw her.

The Sheepeater girl was startled, but not afraid.

He smiled and beckoned to her.

He appeared to be friendly, she thought. And her people were not at war with his, Tamanmo had told her.

Still, she was not so courageous as to be led by his beckoning.

She stood unmoving, but she returned his smile.

He moved toward her, and for a moment she had the urge to flee.

But his voice held her. She could not understand his words, but they had a soothing, friendly sound. Words like you might use when approaching a pony.

A pony you intended to mount, she thought. And at that instant fear struck her.

She turned and started to run, but tripped,

slowing enough that he dove and grabbed her legs and felled her. Kicking wildly, she loosened his grasp and struggled to her knees. She was gaining her feet when his fist caught her below her right ear, driving her to the ground once more.

She was stunned, but got herself turned to face him.

A barrage of blows smashed into her features, sending her sprawling on her back. His hard fists hammered away as he straddled her body.

She felt her cheekbones breaking and her mouth destroyed.

Until finally he stopped and ripped up her skirt, and forced himself into her.

It was the last thing she ever felt.

CHAPTER NINE

It was Ella who discovered the body. She was in shock when she returned to the encampment. Initially unable to speak, she stood, staring vacantly from one man to another, until her eyes came to rest on the figure of Sandow.

He was seated against the trunk of a pine, busily wiping dust from parts of his revolver. She saw dried blood on his knuckles, something apparently none of the others had yet noticed. There was also a scratch on his cheek.

Instinctively, she sought out Seaver, passing by Pandre and Dorsey to reach him.

She usually avoided him, and at her approach he gave her a curious look.

'Mr Seaver, I've got to talk to you,' she said quietly.

'Yes?'

Then she did something he thought was strange. She grasped his arm and led him to the fringe of the clearing away from the others.

'What's the problem?' he said.

She raised her hand and pointed into the timber toward where she had come.

'Back there,' she said.

'Back there, what?'

'An Indian girl,' she said.

'They using women to spy on us now?' he said. 'They must be losing their concern about us.'

'She's been killed.'

'*Killed?*'

'Raped, I think. Her skirt torn off.'

'Raped?'

'Her face beaten in,' she said. 'Oh, my God! It's terrible!'

'Show me,' he said.

Without a word, she started into the trees. He followed at her heels.

They came upon the scene, and she halted a few yards away from the body. He could see it

82

lying there and knew she wasn't going any closer.

He said then what came into his mind. 'Indians sometimes deal harsh punishment to their women.'

'No!' she said. 'It was Sandow!'

'How do you know?' He turned to give her a sharp look.

'I *know!*' she said.

He shook his head slightly, turned away, and strode to where the body lay.

For a long time he stood there staring down at it. And suddenly he knew she was right.

He turned away, sick. Then came the rage, a rage to kill the one who had committed this horror. A rage against Sandow.

He said to Ella, 'Come on,' and started backtrailing toward the camp.

She hurried to follow in his footsteps, as if terrified of being left alone with the body.

Dorsey looked up to see them returning together, and his face took on a quizzical look.

Seaver strode up to him.

'What's up?' Dorsey said.

'There's an Indian girl's body back there,' Seaver said.

'Indian girl?'

'Beaten to death,' Seaver said.

'Show me.'

*   *   *

83

Dorsey stared, as Seaver had done.

Finally he said, 'Sandow?'

Seaver remained silent.

Dorsey said then, 'First, we'd best bury her. Get her hidden from the Indians.'

'No,' Seaver said. 'Do you think you can hide a grave from Indian eyes?'

'We've got to try.'

'No,' Seaver said. 'That's not the way.'

'What then?'

'Send Pandre as an emmissary. Offer to turn the girl's killer over to them.'

Dorsey looked shocked. 'Turn Sandow over to them? God, Seaver, don't you know what they'll do to him?'

'I know.'

'They'll torture him for hours, days maybe, until he dies.'

'Look at that girl's body,' Seaver said. 'Hardly more than a kid. He'll get what he deserves from them.'

Dorsey said, 'No, he's ridden with me and my men. He's one of us.'

'Look at the girl there,' Seaver said again.

'He deserves death,' Dorsey said. 'I agree. But we'll give him a court-martial and hang him.'

'Not good enough,' Seaver said.

Dorsey went on, as if giving orders, 'We'll hang him and leave him for those Sheepeaters to do with what they may. But I will not turn over a live man of my command to Indian

84

torture.'

'You're not an officer any more,' Seaver said.

'He's still in my command, Seaver. He'll have his trial, and his sentence will be carried out.'

'A hanging may not be enough to satisfy their vengeance, *Captain*.'

Dorsey's face hardened. 'It will have to do,' he said.

'You are a fool if you think so.'

'I'm saying how it will be.'

'Then we'd best get on with it. Quick justice may save our own hides. First though, you've got to send your other men here to view the corpse.'

'I'll bring them myself.'

'Who'll guard Sandow?'

Dorsey was silent, then said, 'Give me your word you'll not take off with Miss Gordon, and I'll return your gun.'

'Fair enough.'

'And he gets his trial, you understand? Don't try taking justice into your own hands.'

'I'll be sorely tempted,' Seaver said. 'But I agree.'

*   *   *

They returned to the clearing, Dorsey with his gun drawn.

Sandow still had his own disassembled and

was cleaning it, as if he had to do something to keep himself occupied. The gun didn't need cleaning, it had not been used.

At Dorsey's order, he handed it over, strangely without protest.

Dorsey went to a saddlebag, threw it in, and drew forth Seaver's. He took it over to Seaver and handed it to him.

Bunce and Griffin, as well as Pandre, watched curiously. Dorsey said to them, 'Come on. You too, Indian.'

Dorsey started back into the timber, and with puzzled expressions they followed.

Ella drew close to Seaver, her face still white and looking ill.

'What the hell is going on?' Sandow said. His tone sounded conversational.

Seaver did not bother to reply.

There was a period of silence. Then Sandow said, 'Damn fool Injun wench! She had to try to fight me off. I only wanted to make pleasure with her. For her as well as me.'

Seaver was silent, but Ella began to cry softly.

'She kicked at me,' Sandow said. 'Tried to bite me, tried to scratch out my eyes. Made me lose my head, you know?'

Seaver said nothing.

'I wish now I hadn't done it,' Sandow said. 'One thing just led to another, you know?'

This time, Seaver said harshly, 'I don't know at all.'

'What they going to do after they look at her?' Sandow asked nervously.

'They're going to give you a trial,' Seaver said.

Sandow seemed to relax a bit. Then he said, 'Okay, then. They'll understand when I tell them how it come about.'

Seaver said, 'You stupid, rotten son of a bitch!'

*   *   *

The others came back, the three whites looking pale and shaken. Pandre's face was hard set, and his eyes had a bitter look.

Dorsey sat them on the ground, he and Griffin and Bunce side by side, Sandow a few feet away facing them.

He left Seaver and Ella and Pandre at a distance behind Sandow.

It took a moment for Seaver to recognize the placement: Dorsey had approximated the seating arrangement of a court-martial.

It occurred to Seaver that Dorsey had personal experience in such placings since he himself had been court-martialed.

Now Dorsey spoke. 'Sandow, you are accused of killing that Indian girl back there in the timber. What do you have to say?'

'Just what I told Seaver here,' Sandow said. 'I wanted to pleasure us together, and she fought me off, and I lost my head and hit her a few licks. Wasn't my intention that she up and died.'

'You admit that you killed her?' Dorsey said.

'I admit she up and died after I hit her, and it wasn't my intention. She brought it on herself.'

'I warned you when you attacked Miss Gordon,' Dorsey said. 'You ignored my warning and attacked the Indian girl. You are found guilty of murder, and sentenced to hang by your neck until dead.'

Sandow looked shocked, but said nothing more.

They brought up a horse and got him mounted, hands tied and a noose around his neck. The hang rope was fastened to a tree limb. A tether rope was tied to a nearby trunk and to the horse's bridle to keep the gelding from running away when they slapped his haunch.

Dorsey stood beside the horse, his hat in his hand. He looked up at Sandow and met his eyes, and said, 'Have you got any last words you want to say?'

Sandow said, 'I'm sorry it happened.'

He let his glance sweep the faces of the others then, and saw no expressions on them.

He shrugged, turned back to Dorsey, and said, 'I've always been a good gunhand for you, Dorsey.'

'So?' Dorsey said.

'You might consider this: Them Injuns may

be a sight put out about the Injun girl, even though it was an accident, like I said.'

'That has occurred to me,' Dorsey said.

'So,' Sandow said, 'you might consider again before you hang me. You're going to be outnumbered by far. And you'll need every gunhand you can get.'

'I have considered that.'

'And?'

'And this!' Dorsey said, and slapped his hat hard against the horse's rump.

The mount shot forward until the tether jerked it to a halt.

The drop did not break Sandow's neck, and he hung there writhing, his head twisted grotesquely, his eyes bulging.

Ella fainted.

*　　　*　　　*

It was one of the Sheepeater squaws who went to Tamanmo and told him that the girl was missing.

'The bold one?' he said.

'Yes,' the squaw said. 'The same.'

'I will look for her,' Tamanmo said.

He remembered she had shown curiosity about the whites, and set off immediately toward their camp, on foot.

He picked up her trail, and as he drew near the campsite, he found her body.

A terrible rage came upon him then. He had

89

his rifle with him, and he had a craving to use it. After a brief and anguished pause, he continued on. As he neared the camp he noted the silence and judged it had been abandoned.

Closing in cautiously, he sighted the hanging corpse. He stood staring at it for a time, searching his mind for what its presence meant. After deciding it had not been left as some kind of bait for a trap, he approached it.

He studied the dried blood on the knuckles of both hands. He looked at the face held bloated by the tourniquet stricture of the noose, and saw the fingernail gouge on the left cheek. The girl would have fought back, he was sure. And suddenly he knew. This was the one who had killed her.

His conclusion was hard for him to believe. *The whites had dealt out this punishment to one of their own for the girl's death?*

He turned away slowly and retraced his steps to where the girl lay.

What if they had? It was not enough. They should have prevented its happening.

They should not have been here in the first place.

This was Sheepeater country.

The whites were intruders. And for this he would make them pay.

First, though, he brought his band to view the girl's body, then, postponing its burial under a cairn, he took them to the hanging corpse of her killer.

There, to the wailing squaws, armed with knives, he gestured his approval.

Their wails became screams of rage as they attacked the body, slashing and stabbing and cutting chunks from it to throw on the ground and stomp.

Two close relatives shoved each other to tear away the pants and bare the genitals. Then one grasped and drew them taut while the other sawed them free and tossed them to a waiting dog.

Their screams and wailing rose in volume, so great that the white party, now hurrying on its way at several miles distance, heard the echoes of it against the walls of a canyon.

'What is that?' Ella asked Seaver.

'They've found the girl,' he said. 'And now they've found Sandow hanging there. And they've turned loose their squaws to take vengeance on his body, I reckon.'

'Do you think that will satisfy them?'

'No,' he said. 'That's just the beginning.'

'What will we do?'

'You see that escarpment up ahead? I'm hoping we can reach it before they catch up. We've got a chance to hold them off from there.'

'For how long?'

'Ah,' he said, 'that, Miss Gordon, is the question.'

*   *   *

They reached the foot of the escarpment and began the climb. As Seaver had noted earlier, the slope was spotted with rocky outcroppings that offered scattered cover against enemy fire.

After they gained a little height, he called a halt.

'We'll settle in here and wait,' he said.

Dorsey wasn't sure it was the thing to do. 'We could be making miles while we're sitting here.'

'They will make a quick strike,' Seaver said, 'now that they've found the girl's body. I'm counting on that. This is a natural fort. If we push on now they'll have us with less protection.'

'We'll have to leave sooner or later,' Dorsey said.

'Better later, my way of thinking. Here we've got a chance to cut down on some of the odds. At least see how many we're up against. See what they're armed with.'

Pandre, listening, spoke up. 'They don't quit with one attack. Not after they see the girl dead.'

'Like I said,' Seaver said, 'it's a chance to cut down the odds.'

'You mean, to kill off more Indians, Mr Seaver,' Ella said. 'Why don't you say so? Those Indians have justification to feel the way they do.'

'I do not question their justification, ma'am,' Seaver said. 'I do object to dying to

92

avenge a crime I didn't commit.'

She said, 'Aren't parleys sometimes held? To try to work out the differences between opposing forces?' She did not look at Seaver when she asked. She directed her question to Dorsey.

'That's true, ma'am,' Dorsey said. 'However, in this case I would judge it wouldn't work. They aren't apt to listen to reason.'

She was not to be put off, and said, 'Pandre, couldn't you act as an emissary?'

'Me?' Pandre said.

'Talk to them. They speak Shoshonean, too. Explain what happened.'

'They know what happened,' Pandre said coldly. 'They don't listen to talk now.' He pointed down into the canyon they had recently left.

A bunch of Indian riders had just emerged from a scatter of timber. They halted, searching the slope and seeing the tethered mounts of the whites, only partly hidden among the rocks.

They were four or five hundred yards away, too far for effective shooting.

'Let them attack,' Dorsey said. 'They've got a long open space to cover.'

Griffin said, 'We ought to take a damn good toll on their first charge. Maybe that'll change their minds.'

'That,' Bunce said, 'I'm looking forward to.'

Ella's anger flared. 'You bloodthirsty animals! Can't you see why they feel wronged?'

'Why, yes, ma'am,' Bunce said. 'But they want a fight, we'll sure give them one.'

'But I don't want to see them die!' She turned toward Pandre. 'You shouldn't either. They are cousins to you! Please try to parley.'

Pandre looked thoughtful, and after a short silence, he said, 'For you, Ella, I do this thing.'

Dorsey, hearing this, said to Seaver, 'What do you think?'

'If the Shoshone here is willing, it might be worth a try. In a fight, we'll probably take losses as well as give them.'

Dorsey produced an empty grub sack from his saddlebag, and handed it to Pandre. He also handed him the rifle they had taken from him.

'Tie that on the barrel,' Dorsey said. 'Been a long time since it was white, but it'll have to do.'

Pandre did so, then untethered his mount and got into the saddle. He said then to Ella, 'For you and me, Ella.'

He kicked the horse then, and started riding down the slope, holding up the improvised truce flag so the Sheepeaters could see it.

The whites all waited edgily, wondering if the Sheepeaters would honor a makeshift white flag.

'Damn Injun's got guts,' Griffin said.

Seaver was silent. He agreed with that, but

other thoughts were running through his mind.

Something bothered him.

Pandre kept riding, now out of effective range of the men above. But still none of the Sheepeaters rode forth to meet him.

Pandre halted, seemed to call something to the waiting Indians.

Then, after a moment, he moved forward again, and rode on till he reached them.

There was another pause.

Ella said eagerly, 'They are going to parley!'

And, even as she spoke, the Sheepeaters turned and disappeared into the timber.

Taking Pandre with them.

That's when Seaver swore.

*　　　*　　　*

Chris Carter knew a battle was imminent and from a distant rise he waited expectantly. He was behind the Sheepeaters, reading sign of much that was going on.

He had not been close enough to witness the fate of the Sheepeater girl, but he later came upon her burial cairn, and upon the still-hanging remnants of a corpse, which he identified as one of Dorsey's men.

He recognized the mutilation as Indian handiwork and guessed there must be a connection between the two deaths. A connection that could be an indication of trouble to come for the rest of the Dorsey

95

party.

He had left the corpse hanging and hurried on.

He had watched the whites fort up behind the high rocks of a slope, and the Sheepeater band of braves gather below.

Then he saw the lone Indian emerge from among the whites and ride down to the Sheepeaters with an improvised peace flag held aloft.

CHAPTER TEN

In a small clearing, a few yards from the timber's edge, the Sheepeaters halted.

The Indian chieftain said, 'I am Tamanmo, leader of this band of the Tukuarikas. You are Shoshone?'

Pandre nodded. 'I am Pandre, of the Shoshone. Sometimes of the Duck Valley reservation set up for us by the whites.'

'Why are you here, in our land?' Tamanmo said. 'And riding with these whites?'

'They took me prisoner.'

'And now they let you go?'

'They sent me to parley for them because we have a common language.'

'You come to ask for peace? We have reason for war.'

Pandre shook his head. His nodding and

96

shaking of the head was instinctive now, long ago picked up from the whites at the mission school. 'I know. They ask for peace. I do not. Not for them. Only for the white woman and myself.'

'We saw the white woman,' Tamanmo said. 'And what is she to you?'

'I know her from Duck Valley,' Pandre said. 'I stole her to be my woman.'

Tamanmo studied him without expression. But some of the others, watching and listening, smirked faintly. There was some muttered comment among them.

Tamanmo said then, 'And she is willing?'

'I will make her willing' Pandre said.

There was a further muttering among the others, this time of male approval.

'Why do you choose a white woman?' Tamanmo said.

'Why does any brave choose his woman?' Pandre answered.

'Many times it is a mistake,' Tamanmo said, and paused. Then he added, 'So you want to join us to get your woman back?'

'It is my wish.'

Tamanmo studied him closely. 'Tell me. Why did they hang one of their own kind?'

Pandre hesitated, giving thought to his answer before he spoke. Then he said, 'They are whites. They thought that by killing the girl's attacker, it would satisfy your desire for vengeance.'

'It is not enough. They are fools to think so.'

'That is the way whites are,' Pandre said.

'You have a rifle. You will fight with us to exterminate them to give a proper revenge?'

'I will fight beside you. To get free, with my woman.'

Tamanmo glanced at the Winchester held by Pandre. The grub bag still hung limply from the barrel. 'Your weapon is loaded?'

'I do not know. Their leader handed it to me.'

'You took a chance riding to us with an empty rifle.'

'It was my chance to get away to join you.'

'No matter. We have bullets for it.'

'I was hoping so,' Pandre said.

Tamanmo met his eyes and the stare held long between them, and then Tamanmo said, 'All right. But I will be watching you. You understand?'

'As I would, in your place,' Pandre said. 'But you will find you have chosen wisely. I know these whites.'

'Check your weapon, then,' Tamanmo said. 'We are about to attack.'

Pandre did so, and found it loaded, and was surprised that the ex-army officer had not sent him off helpless. Dorsey was a fool, Pandre thought, for that. Still, it said something for the man.

He frowned.

Tamanmo, watching, saw his frown and

98

said, 'You are not happy it is loaded?'

Pandre said quickly, 'Of course I am. It is just that I did not expect him to be so—foolish.'

'Foolish, eh? Either that or he trusted you.' It was the Sheepeater chieftain's turn to frown.

'I never gave him reason to,' Pandre said.

'Are you ready to attack with us?'

'No.'

'No?'

'I say so because I have been up there. They are ready and waiting, protected by the rocks. They are eager for you to try the attack. Because they will shoot you dead before you can cover half the distance.'

'What do you suggest?'

'They carry only canteens, which they filled at the last creek behind us. But up among those bare rocks it will not last long. There is no spring up there where they are. Let us wait them out here. When their water is gone they will have to move from their natural fort. Then we can pursue, catch them somewhere beyond.'

'You are familiar with warfare?' Tamanmo said.

'No. But I am familiar with these whites—enough to guess what they will do.' Pandre paused. 'But the decision is yours. You are the chief. If you say attack. I will attack with you.'

The Sheepeater was silent, thinking. He glanced around at his men. They awaited his order.

It bothered him that this Shoshone newcomer had suggested a different plan than his own. He had a feeling that the Shoshone was right, yet he felt the stares of his braves on him. He feared to lose face.

'The rocks are smaller on the slope from here to where they are,' Tamanmo said. 'But some are big enough to give cover to a man. We will leave our horses here. We will attack on foot, charging from rock to rock.'

Pandre said nothing.

'What do you think of that, Shoshone?'

'You are the chief,' Pandre said. 'I will follow.'

'No.'

'No?'

'You will be out front,' Tamanmo said. 'You will lead the charge. It is a great honor.' His expression feigned sincerity.

Pandre heard the chuckling of the other braves.

*　　　*　　　*

From up on the escarpment, the whites watched them coming.

Ella was the first to speak, crying out, 'That's Pandre out in front! Don't shoot!'

Dorsey said, 'Ma'am, I'm afraid your Indian has switched sides.'

'But he wouldn't!'

100

'Doesn't look like he's being driven,' Seaver said.

'He must be!'

Bunce said, 'Lady, you in love with that Injun?'

'Of course not!' she said. 'But we were friends.'

'I thought he kidnapped you,' Griffin said.

'He did. But even so, he didn't treat me badly.'

'Could be we rescued you before he got around to that,' Dorsey said.

He said to the others then, 'Don't fire until I give the order.'

The Indians were working their way up from rock to rock, but were not yet within rifle range. Suddenly one of them half rose from cover and sent a bullet that kicked up dirt a hundred yards below the whites.

'See?' Ella said. 'Pandre isn't shooting.'

'Got more sense than the one that did,' Dorsey said. 'That was just a bullet wasted.'

'I don't think he'll shoot at all,' she said.

They were all silent at that.

'Please don't shoot him,' she said. 'The others, if you must, but not him.'

The men exchanged glances. None of them spoke, but it was plain enough there was an understanding among them.

Dorsey said then, 'Ma'am, have you ever handled a firearm?'

'No!'

He had an extra rifle lying beside him. 'Here's your chance to learn. This is Sandow's.'

She looked over at him as he held up the weapon.

'It's loaded,' he said. 'You cock it by levering the handle down and up. You sight down the barrel, pointing at your target. Then you squeeze the trigger.'

'I don't want it,' she said.

Dorsey shrugged. 'Just in case you do,' he said, and laid it down beside her. 'I tell you that, ma'am, because I have seen firsthand what Indians sometimes do to white woman captives.'

'Pandre would never let them hurt me!' she said.

He met that comment with silence, just looking at her with no expression on his face.

That lack of expression and the silence gradually made her feel foolish. She said, 'I know you are concerned.'

'Yes, ma'am,' he said.

After a moment, he turned his attention once again to the steadily advancing Sheepeaters.

Pandre was still a little ahead of the others.

*　　*　　*

In Pandre's mind there was conflict. It was an old one, going back to his early days at the mission school. A conflict between the white

102

culture he had been exposed to, and his Indian heritage.

He had known half-breeds who lived with this war within. It was a conflict that could sometimes cause erratic behavior.

And, though he had no white blood, he was torn by the same split feelings as he neared a point on the escarpment that put him in firing range.

The whites he was about to fire upon had done him no wrong, apart from intruding upon his plan to take Ella as his woman.

Even Seaver, who was out to take her away from him, had indicated no intention of taking him in for arrest.

At that moment, he did not know if he was going to open the attack or not. Still undecided, he raised his head slightly to peer over his rocky cover.

A shot came from above.

It struck him high, bowling him over so that he sprawled on his back, exposed now on the slope.

Ella cried, 'Oh, no!'

Everyone could see the blood welling from the bullet hole drilled in Pandre's forehead.

'He wasn't even shooting,' Ella said.

'In battle, Miss Gordon,' Dorsey said, 'there is no set procedure for who dies when the shooting starts.'

'Who shot him?' There was agony in her voice.

There was a silence, then Bunce said, 'Why, I did, ma'am.'

'But why?'

'Because he was out there,' Bunce said, 'and about to shoot at us.'

'I can't believe that!'

'No ma'am. You don't want to believe it,' Bunce said.

The Sheepeaters were now within range, and opened up with a barrage that sent bullets ricocheting off the boulders of the rampart.

'Stay down,' Seaver said to Ella. 'One of those bullets could take your head just the way it took Pandre's.'

'You don't even care,' she said.

'About him? No, ma'am, him I don't.' He hesitated a moment, then said, 'I do care what happens to you.'

'Because there's a reward for me,' she said.

'That too, of course.'

There was more firing, halting any further comment she might have made.

The Sheepeaters made their charge, leapfrogging from rock to rock, giving no more than a glimpse before dropping from sight again.

The whites were snap-shooting, confused by the quickness of a dozen random targets that gave no clue as to which would appear where.

This terrain was Sheepeater habitat, Seaver thought. Long years of hunting mountain sheep among lofty crags in earlier times, with

104

only bow and arrow, seemed to have given them the surefooted mobility of the sheep themselves.

Suddenly high on the shoulder of the escarpment an Indian came over the rise, not fifty yards away. He halted there, unseen by the whites, behind and slightly above them.

Their eyes were all searching the rocky cover below, intent on catching a target among the elusively advancing foe.

At the insistence of Seaver, Ella had withdrawn slightly from the breastwork.

'Too many ricochets flying around,' he'd told her. 'Take that rifle of Sandow's and get back a ways.'

Stung by his curt command, but unnerved by the whining bullets, she had obeyed. She crouched there, fearful, but some instinct caused her to turn. Ella saw the Indian kneeling with rifle raised and pointed at Seaver.

Without thought, she lifted the weapon she was holding, levered it, pointed it at the Indian, and fired just as he noticed her, his eyes showing his surprise.

She saw him fall backward as her bullet struck him in the face, sending him tumbling out of sight below the rise.

Seaver whirled about at the sound of her shot and saw her lower the rifle.

He called out, 'What was it?'

She faced him and said, 'Indian. He was

going to shoot you.'

She dropped the rifle, leaned over, and began to retch.

*   *   *

Tamanmo felt the enormous pain of the woman's bullet as it smashed his cheekbone, passing through.

But that pain was nothing compared to the excruciating bone splinter that pierced his eye.

His right eye. The one he had been sighting with down the barrel of his weapon.

The eye needed for hunting. A Sheepeater who could not hunt was nothing.

That was the thought in his mind as he passed out from the pain.

*   *   *

At a hundred and fifty yards, the Sheepeaters had come to the edge of the lower rocky area.

Between them and the defenders above, there was only sparse cover of a thrust of boulders here and there.

They halted.

This was where Pandre had been when he had been shot.

A young brave who had never taken part before in the earlier Sheepeater conflicts against whites took refuge close to Pandre's body, studying it carefully.

He could not take his eyes off the shattered skull and scattered brains of the dead Shoshone. All the will to continue the charge up the slope suddenly deserted him.

He turned away and looked at the open expanse ahead, and a panic took him. Glancing over at the brave nearest to him, he called out, and when the brave turned, he pointed out the near-headless corpse.

The other brave was young too, and his face took on a look like that of the first one.

Slightly below the pair were the others, waiting on the two in front to move.

The first of the young braves yelled to the other. 'Where is Tamanmo?'

The other called, 'He was below.'

'He should be up here leading.'

From just below, an older brave called, 'I was below when he told me he was going to come at them from the side.'

That seemed to anger the first young brave, and he called back, 'Then we will wait until we see what success he has.'

The older brave was silent. He did not answer one way or another.

*   *   *

Behind the rampart, Seaver was looking down at them. He said, 'They don't like that open stretch, and I can't blame them for that.'

Just as he said it, a brave rose from behind

107

the third rock down and fired. He dropped from sight again, and a fusilade erupted from both sides.

*   *   *

The sound of the rifle fire brought Tamanmo around.

With consciousness came the awful agony of the bone splinter in his eye. It drove him to his feet, started him staggering down the shoulder of the escarpment, half-blind and irrational, but vaguely retracing his way toward where he had abandoned the charge so as to attempt his rear-flank offensive.

In his delirium he had picked up his rifle and still carried it, his other hand pressed over his blinded eye.

He had no thought of using the weapon now; he carried it by habit.

He was driven by instinct to rejoin his men, seeking aid to relieve his pain.

One conscious thought entered the back of his mind: It was the white woman who had shot him, the white woman who had destroyed his eye.

He reached the point where he had left the charge, and found his men had advanced upward. Now, still seeking solace for his wound, he weakly began the climb toward them.

Eventually he reached the nearest one, an

older brave.

The brave whirled about, sensing him beside him, erect and exposed to any lucky shot from above.

He saw the blood flowing from the chieftain's face, even as he grasped at Tamanmo's rifle to pull him down into cover.

'Tamanmo!' he cried.

At the sound of his name, Tamanmo seemed to come out of his shock. 'My eye,' he said.

The brave did not know what comment to make. Then he said, 'At the top they are stopped by the guns of the whites.'

'For now,' Tamanmo said, 'I have lost my taste for battle.' He paused, then said, 'Pass the word up to the others to withdraw.'

'Withdraw, Tamanmo?'

'Withdraw,' Tamanmo said. 'I will launch another attack when I am rid of this pain the woman gave me.'

'The *woman*?' the brave said.

'Call the word upward as I told you. The battle is over for now.'

The old brave was not reluctant to do so. He raised his voice and yelled the order to the next brave above him.

A moment later he could hear this one passing the order up to a pair above. These, in turn, repeated it.

*　　　*　　　*

From above, the whites saw the withdrawal begin.

As the braves rose and started dashing in a reverse leapfrog of their earlier movement, Dorsey's men got off a couple of shots.

One of the braves went down, then got up and resumed running, limping badly.

Griffin kept firing at him, but missed.

'Hold it!' Dorsey said. 'They've had enough.'

'Why?' Griffin said.

'Because that's an order!'

'I mean, why've they had enough?'

Seaver said, 'I saw a brave, bleeding from the face, walk up to the rear line. Maybe he was the chief. Maybe he gave the order.'

Ella said, 'I saw him, too. It's too far away to be sure, but I think he might be the one I shot a while ago up here.'

Dorsey gave her a quick look. 'Lady, you just may have won the battle for us.'

They watched the Indians gather at the bottom, then mount up and ride away eastward.

Seaver went to where Ella said the Indian she had shot had fallen. He came back and said, 'He walked away. But he left blood behind.'

'Oh, God!' Ella said. 'I'm glad I didn't kill him!'

Seaver said, 'Time to head west. We can build up a lead before they decide to attack again.'

'Do you think they will?' Ella said.

'I'm almost sure of it. If that was the chief called them off, he did it for a reason. But that doesn't mean he's giving up.'

'They left Pandre lying down there,' she said. 'Can we bury him?'

The men looked at her, then at one another. When Dorsey's and Seaver's glances met, they held.

Griffin said, 'Bury a damn Injun? An enemy, at that?'

Ella said, 'He was once a friend.'

'To who? To you, maybe.'

Seaver said to Dorsey, 'She saved my life. And she may have won the battle here with that single shot she fired. I say she deserves us granting her whim.'

'It's not a whim!' she said. 'It's human decency.'

'Dorsey?' Seaver said.

'All right,' Dorsey said. 'Anything for the lady.'

'I ain't digging in any rocky soil like this,' Griffin said.

'Besides,' Bunce said, 'we got no tools to dig with.'

'We can cover him with a cairn,' Seaver said.

With the four men fetching rocks, and Ella helping too, it didn't take long.

In a half hour they had it done. Neither Griffin nor Bunce jibed her about it. They seemed to be considering what she had

111

possibly done by shooting the Indian who had appeared behind them, as described by Seaver.

Finished with the cairn, they mounted their horses in silence and, Seaver in the lead, headed westerly again.

Ella rode second behind him.

*   *   *

At the Sheepeater encampment, the old brave who had passed the withdrawal order to the others finally extracted the bone splinter from Tamanmo's eyeball.

This brought some relief of his agony, but even with the swelling the others could see that the Chief's once handsome face would be permanently mutilated.

Some of the younger squaws seemed more perturbed by this than were Tamanmo's braves.

One of the braves thoughtlessly brought a steel pocket mirror once owned by some cavalryman and handed it to him.

With his left eye, he studied his reflection, and they witnessed the rage that momentarily erased the pain from his expression.

With an oath he threw the mirror on the ground.

The old brave, foolishly bold with his years, was the only one who dared a question at that moment, saying, 'Will we let the whites get away?'

'We will *not!*' Tamanmo said. 'And most of all I want the woman! And I want her alive. As soon as I can ride I will get revenge for what she has done to me. Do you not know that this eye is forever blinded? Before she dies, I will wreak the same on her!'

CHAPTER ELEVEN

The whites reached a pass that led between moderately high twin peaks and descended into a valley. Thick stands of yellow pine hid what lay ahead until the group abruptly burst into a meadow.

Seaver halted in surprise. Before them, on a large, flowing creek, was a crude sprawl of shacks of undressed timber, and along the banks he saw, here and there, installations of placer-mining equipment.

'By god!' he said. 'A mining camp.'

Dorsey said, 'I didn't know there were any.'

'I hope they got some whiskey,' Bunce said.

Griffin said, 'And some town grub. I'm getting damn sick of living off game.'

Ella, who seldom made a rejoinder to either man, now said, 'Lord, I hope so!'

'We'll soon find out,' Dorsey said. He pulled up beside Seaver, and together they led the way into the single narrow street.

There was a hitchrack in front of a place with

a porch. It looked like it might be a saloon or a store or maybe both. There was a pair of doors made of rough lumber, held open by a couple of rocks.

Seaver and Dorsey swung down, tied their mounts, and stepped up on the porch.

Dorsey said to the others still in the saddle, 'Wait here till we check this out.'

Inside, they saw a crude bar and, behind it, a man, maybe in his late forties, with a trimmed graying beard. He wore no apron; was instead dressed in typical miner's garb and suspenders.

He scrutinized the pair of strangers. Seaver returned the stare.

Dorsey said, 'You selling?'

'Selling what? Whiskey?' There wasn't much friendliness in the words.

Dorsey had seen the canned goods on the opposite side of the room and said, 'Foodstuff, too.'

'Some, maybe. For a price. I carry my stock for the men who mine here. I got to have it all packed in, so it ain't cheap.'

'Packed in how far?' Seaver asked.

'More than a hundred miles, I'd say. By rugged trail.'

'How far as a crow flies?' Dorsey said.

'Half that, maybe.'

'Where from?'

'Moose City,' the man behind the bar said. 'You know the place?'

'Heard of it,' Seaver said.

114

'It ain't much of a place, either,' the barman said.

'We've got money,' Dorsey said.

'In that case,' the barman said, reaching down. He brought up a bottle and set it on the bar. 'This'll cost you a dollar a drink.'

'I got two men outside,' Dorsey said.

'Bring them in.'

'And a woman,' Seaver said.

'A woman? By geez! That could mean trouble around here. Ain't seen nothing but an Injun squaw here in over a year.' The barman set out five glasses in front of them.

'What tribe?' Seaver said.

'Wasn't no tribe come. Just her wandered in, following a pack train. Set up her lone camp over on the edge of the meadow. Come here to peddle herself to the men hereabouts. Nez Percé, she said she was.'

'I reckon they were glad to see her.'

'That they were, friend. That they were. But not for long. Wasn't but a short spell before half the camp come down with the clap. They'd have hung her if she hadn't seen the writing on the wall and run off ahead of a lynch party.'

'Woman with us is white,' Dorsey said. 'High-class lady.'

'She peddling?'

Seaver was suddenly angered. 'Listen, you! This is a *lady*!' In his anger, he then said something that shocked himself. 'She's *my* woman, you understand?'

115

The barman took a step backward out of reach. 'Hell, man, I didn't know! I didn't mean no offense.'

Seaver felt Dorsey's stare on him and shifted his glance to the ex-officer. He half-expected to see amused surprise there, but he didn't.

He saw instead a scowl, as if Dorsey didn't like what he'd heard.

As if Dorsey figured he had a claim of his own on Ella.

Trying to make amends for his blunder, the barman said, 'Bring your folks in, if that's your inclination. The lady is welcome, too. Might be she'd have an eye for some of them canned goods on the shelves over there.'

Dorsey went to the doorway and gestured for the others to come in.

Seaver said to the barman, 'You ever have trouble with Sheepeater Indians hereabouts?'

'Never,' the barman said. 'Not since the war, way back in seventy-nine.'

'Were you here then?'

'Not here. Hell, these diggings come afterward. But I was in the war. Private Kelly, that was me. That's how I come to see the country. Liked it so well I come back after discharge from Howard's army. Went to prospecting for a long spell. Them Sheepeaters never caused no trouble once they gave up. I think most of them was sent to the Fort Hall reservation.'

'Not all of them,' Seaver said.

116

At that moment, Griffin and Bunce came in, followed by Ella, who was escorted by Dorsey.

Kelly took one look at Ella, quickly removed one glass from the bar, and returned it to a shelf behind him. 'She ain't the kind to drink in a saloon, for sure,' he said to Seaver.

'Glad you realize that,' Seaver said.

'Easy enough to see,' Kelly said. He paused, then said, 'What did you mean about all the Sheepeaters not being gone? There's always been a few roaming hunters and their families that avoided being took. But all the years I been here, they never bothered us none. Never even made contact.'

The men were now passing the bottle around, filling their glasses. Ella had gone over to scan the shelves of edibles.

Bunce tossed down his drink and said, 'Mister, you been damn lucky if that's so.'

'What do you mean?'

'I mean them bastards tried to kill us off a while back.'

'That don't make sense,' Kelly said. 'Why would they want to kill you?'

Bunce seemed to realize he'd made a mistake. It took him a bit before he answered. 'Hell, Injuns don't need a reason, I reckon.'

'I don't understand.' Kelly kept staring at Bunce as if he expected further explanation.

Bunce exchanged glances with Dorsey, then said, 'I don't have no other answer for it. Why do you care?'

117

'I care,' Kelly said, 'because we ain't had Injun trouble for all these years. But I remember how it was when we was fighting them, and I don't want them stirred up again.'

The others were all silent, and Kelly went on, 'Hell, man, you can see this little camp would be sitting ducks for any Injuns on the warpath.'

Dorsey drew some money from his pocket and laid it on the bar. 'We'll have another round,' he said.

Temporarily distracted from talk about the Indians, Kelly poured the drinks and picked up the money to pay for them.

But the distraction was brief. Done with that, he said, 'About them Injuns—'

Seaver interrupted. 'Can you serve up a meal for us?' He gestured across the room toward Ella. 'The lady there would sure appreciate it.'

'Well, I guess. I fix up meals now and then. Nothing fancy, you understand. Only for miners tired of cooking their own.'

'Be good enough,' Seaver said.

Kelly looked at the fistful of currency Dorsey had left on the bar. 'All right,' he said. 'I'll be back in the kitchen for a spell.'

When he was gone, Bunce said, 'I didn't figure mention of them Injuns would spook him so.'

Dorsey said, 'I guess he still remembers fighting them back in the war. And, as he says, a camp this size would be hard put to fight off a bunch on the warpath.'

118

Seaver was thoughtful, then said, 'They could put up a stiffer fight than the four of us.'

Ella had come over to them and was listening, Seaver caught her eye and said, 'Even the five of us.'

She frowned, and shook her head. 'No!' she said. 'I couldn't shoot again.'

He was silent, studying her face. 'All right, then,' he said. 'Four of us. And the miners.' He looked at Dorscy. 'This is the place to make a stand if they're on our trail again. Worth laying over a couple of days to find out.' He paused. 'If the Indians come, they'll attack the whole camp. That means we'd have the gold diggers on our side against them. It'd up our chances considerable.'

'That's a cold way of looking at it,' Ella said.

'A cold way is needed here,' Seaver said. 'We lucked out on that set-to on the mountain. It won't likely happen again.'

Griffin spoke up. 'You don't know for sure these gold prospectors would put up a good fight.'

'I'm betting they would. They'd be fighting for their own lives, too. Nobody fights harder than for that.'

'You would jeopardize their lives to save ours?' Ella said.

'Fighting Indians,' Seaver said, 'you use every ally you can get.'

'You are unfair,' she said. She sounded disappointed in him.

He shrugged, then said to Dorsey, 'Well?'

'I admire the lady's reluctance. But, after the things I have done in my life, I can't pretend to be noble. Your idea has its points. I'm for it.'

Seaver said, 'Griffin?'

Griffin said, 'I'm with you.'

Bunce said, 'Me too. I only hope we can bring these gold diggers to side us.'

'They'll bring themselves to it if an attack occurs,' Seaver said. He looked again at Ella. 'The vote is four to one, lady.'

She shook her head. 'You are a hard man,' she said sadly.

'It takes that sometimes to survive,' he said.

She shook her head again, as if she found that difficult to accept.

He understood. He was finding his plan hard to accept, himself. But he couldn't tell her he was driven to this underhanded strategy by his growing feeling toward her and by his memory that she had saved his life back there on the mountain.

*   *   *

Kelly returned with a couple of trays with plates of food. Each plate carried an entree of venison.

'Damn!' Griffin said.

Ella said nothing, simply staring at it.

'What's the matter?' Kelly asked.

Griffin said, 'Was hoping for a change, is all.

120

We been living off game lately.'

'So have we,' Kelly said sharply. 'But you got canned vegetables there too.'

'I ain't complaining,' Griffin said. 'Just stating a fact.'

Kelly looked disgruntled. 'Injuns live on game, mostly.'

'So?' Bunce said. 'Why bring that up?'

'Because you mentioned Injuns. Sounded like you had a run-in with some. If so, I'd like to hear about it. Living out here like we do, any Injun trouble could mean danger to us.'

Bunce looked like he was about to speak, but Seaver beat him to it and said, 'We spotted a few trailing us, over the other side of that range behind us.'

'Probably curious what you're doing in the area,' Kelly said.

'Then came a short set-to as we climbed up the slope.'

'Any casualties?'

Seaver shook his head. 'We were lucky.'

'I mean Sheepeaters.'

'Didn't see any of their bodies lying around,' Seaver said.

Ella was staring at him, and he felt it. He said, 'I guess they didn't intend a serious battle.'

Kelly weighed that, then said, 'After all these years, even a skirmish ain't like them.'

Seaver shrugged.

'I hope they ain't still following you,' the

121

barman said.

'We ain't seen any sign of them since.'

'You're moving right on, ain't you?'

'Figured to lay over a couple of days, rest up our horses,' Seaver said. 'These mountain climbs are kind of hard on them.'

Kelly looked to have a protest on his lips, but Dorsey saw it and pulled out another wad of currency, laying it on the counter.

He said, 'We can advance you money to cover meals and such, if it'd make you feel more hospitable.'

Kelly eyed the greenbacks. He said a little reluctantly, 'It just might. Real money is hard to come by around here. I mostly trade for gold dust.'

'I figured that,' Dorsey said.

'But only for a couple of days, you understand? I got to save my supplies to keep the town going. And it'll be weeks before a pack train is due here.'

'Fair enough,' Dorsey said. 'We'll bivouac here on the edge of the meadow.'

'Bivouac? You got the sound of a army man.'

'Once was,' Dorsey said.

'Officer?'

'That make any difference?'

'Not to me,' the store owner said. 'I was just guessing by the way you speak.'

'Let's leave it that way then,' Dorsey said.

He shoved the currency across the counter

and said, 'This is on account.'

Kelly counted it, folded it, and put it in his pocket.

'Yes, *sir!*' he said.

* * *

They set up camp in the meadow. From there they could see a distance along the creek where men were shoveling sandy soil into sluice boxes. They looked busy as ants.

'How many men did he say was in the camp here?' Bunce said.

'Twenty,' Seaver said.

'Won't do us much good,' Dorsey said, 'if the Indians attack before we have a chance to mobilize them for action.' He paused. 'I'm going to keep a watch posted on our backtrail to warn us.'

There was still a lot of army left in the man, Seaver thought. He had been just about to suggest it.

'We'll rotate the duty,' Dorsey said.

'Fair enough.'

Dorsey went on, 'One of us should alert those gold diggers of a possible attack, so they have weapons ready.'

'It's going to stir up some arguments if they know we're the cause of it,' Seaver said. 'We'll need to downplay our part in it like we did with the store owner.'

Dorsey said, 'I'll talk to them. I'll take Kelly

with me to help.'

'Will he do that?'

'He likes money,' Dorsey said. 'I recognized a kindred spirit there. You noticed how he grabbed the bait I laid on top his bar.' He paused. 'It's a hell of a thing what the lust for money can do to a man's integrity, Seaver.'

'I'm beginning to believe it,' Seaver said.

Ella said, 'Is not the reward offered for my return your own motivation, Mr Seaver?'

'It was.'

'And now?'

He hesitated, then said, 'Lady, I do what I think has to be done. I let that guide me.'

Dorsey interrupted. 'Seaver, you're the man to select a sentry site. Find one and take the first watch. Make it four hours. The Indians won't strike at night. When your time is up, Bunce will take over, followed by Griffin, then myself. Agreed?'

'Agreed,' Seaver said.

'Meanwhile, I'll get Kelly and alert the miners to keep weapons with them until this scare is over.'

'I hope you can convince them.'

'A little more of that bank loot will make Kelly a strong ally. I'll have him do most of the talking. After all, the man who supplies the needs of a camp like this is a man they'll listen to.'

'Make it sound like there's only an outside chance of any trouble,' Seaver said.

'I'll bear that in mind,' Dorsey said.

*   *   *

It all went as planned, except two days passed and there was no sign of the Sheepeaters.

'We'd best be getting on,' Dorsey said. 'Looks like the Indians lost their taste for battle, back there on the mountain.'

'Let's give it another day,' Seaver said. 'Once we leave the town here, we'll be on our own again.'

'One more day then,' Dorsey said. 'Kelly is getting antsy about his supplies. Antsy, too, about the Indians.'

'You're paying him well for what we're getting.'

'Yeah, and it's *my* money, remember.'

'Bank money, ain't it?'

'I risked my neck to get it,' Dorsey said.

'We pull out too soon, and you may risk your neck to lose it,' Seaver said.

'One more day, then.'

*   *   *

The Indians crept close, just before dawn.

Seaver had lengthened the sentry duty to six-hour stints, around the clock, and was the one on guard.

Quiet as the Indians were, he caught their sound and slipped away toward the bivouac

125

area to alert the others.

'They'll attack at first light,' he said to Dorsey.

He aroused the others, and they quickly took positions among the nearest log structures.

Ella, armed again with Sandow's rifle, stayed close to Seaver and Dorsey, near the store.

Bunce and Griffin came over, and Bunce said, 'We got to wake up them gold miners.'

Griffin said, 'A shot will do it.' He raised his rifle as if to fire.

Seaver, within reach of him, grasped the barrel.

'Not now, dammit!'

'It'll warn the diggers,' Griffin said.

'And also the Indians,' Seaver said. 'Lay low until they start the action. A first surprise could be a big advantage.'

'That's right,' Dorsey said. 'They may see our blankets spread over there where we slept, and be fooled into targeting them.'

Griffin said grumpily, 'By god, I hope so.'

The sky to the east was beginning to lighten.

Kelly suddenly appeared from his quarters in the rear of his store, awakened by their voices.

'They're here?' he said.

'They were coming up behind the bivouac area,' Seaver said. 'Could attack any time now. Can you rouse up some of your men?'

126

'Yeah, some. Any shooting will bring out the rest.'

'Do it, then,' Dorsey said.

'Is that an order, Captain?' Kelly said with a trace of sarcasm. But he moved off to obey.

It was not yet full first light in the bivouac area. From where they waited they could now see the rumpled blankets they had left there.

'Gets much lighter,' Dorsey said, 'they won't be fooled.'

'Yeah.' Seaver said.

But even as he spoke, a barrage came from the fringe of timber, and the fire blast of the Indian weapons showed.

Within minutes, the miners were pouring out of their shacks, most in longjohns only, but weapons in hand.

'Hold your fire!' Seaver called to those nearest. 'They'll come closer when they see there's nothing over there. Don't fire till you've got a good target.'

More camp inhabitants took positions, and the Indians, realizing they had been momentarily fooled, changed the direction of their fire.

There was a quick, fierce exchange of shots, uncertain in the remaining gloom, but the whites could see the enemy had left their mounts and were advancing on foot.

But meeting the defensive fire, the Indians retreated from sight. They were apparently unhit, or at least left no wounded behind.

127

In the temporary quiet that followed, one big, heavily-bearded miner, whom Seaver recognized as the one called Bearcat by the others, yelled over to him.

There was rancor in his voice. 'Them Injuns never bothered us none till you showed up. I think you're somehow the cause of this. And by god, I'm going to hold you responsible.'

Just then, the Sheepeaters reopened their attack from surrounding points of cover, and Seaver put the big miner out of his mind as he fought to repulse them.

He was surprised at their tenacity in taking on the whole town. They must have one hell of a rage for revenge, to drive them to this, he was thinking.

It was full light now, and at that moment Ella cried out, 'There! Did you see him? The one without a weapon. The one who seems to be in command. The one I shot! Oh, did you see his face? Half shot away. And as if his eye is missing! Oh, God!'

The reason for the relentless Sheepeater action was clear to Seaver now.

He had seen what Ella had seen. That was the chief. And they had seen close up what her shot had inflicted on the Indian.

Seaver was certain that she was the target of a personal vendetta. She was the target because of what she had done in saving his life.

She kept saying, 'Did you see his face? Oh, God! Did you see what I did to his face?'

'I saw,' Seaver said tightly.

He was himself shocked at the amount of damage she had done with her single shot back there on the mountain.

But there was no more time to think of it.

The exchange of fire was getting heavy.

CHAPTER TWELVE

Ella said, 'I thought they always rode a circle around a town when they attacked.'

She still sounded distraught from viewing the Indian chieftain's demolished face, as if her mind was only half on the present action.

'On the plains sometimes,' Seaver said, searching targets behind the Sheepeater cover. 'But not always. And, as you can see, they couldn't ride around this one, with timber in the way.'

She said, 'I see that now. I guess I don't know much about warfare.'

Seaver said, 'You're learning.'

'It isn't something I want to learn.'

'Not many do. We learn the trade and use it to survive.'

'But will we?' she said.

'Do you want to?'

'Of course I do!'

'Then start using that rifle you're holding.'

When she didn't reply, he risked a glance in

129

her direction and saw the white, drawn look on her face.

He relented then, and said, 'Forget it. Your weapon wouldn't make a difference. Keep covered. Fire only if we're overrun.'

She just stared at him, saying nothing.

A bullet smacked into the building corner above his head, startling him back to the business at hand.

*   *   *

One of Tamanmo's braves said to him, 'There are many more enemy than we counted on. We did not think to fight a whole town.'

'Nor I,' Tamanmo said. 'I had thought to surprise them where they camped and be done with it.'

'So now?'

Tamanmo's mutilated face twisted further in his bitterness, and he said, 'Most of all I want the woman.'

'She is the one who made you blind,' the brave said.

'If one of us can reach her, we will withdraw. I have plans for her that will take some time. I will see her with a face that matches mine. The other vengeance, for our killed sister, can come after.'

'I saw the woman, and a man, run into that store,' the brave said.

'I thought I did, too,' Tamanmo said. Then,

130

with voice rising in hate, he added, 'But with only one eye, I could not be sure.'

'She is there, Tamanmo.'

'Then we will pinpoint our attack on the place,' Tamanmo said.

Near to him, crouched behind a fallen log, was another brave. This one, though firing a rifle, carried a bow and a quiver of arrows on his back.

Some of the Sheepeaters still preferred such a weapon for hunting in the forests. Game missed by a rifle shot could drive all other game from an area. But a silent arrow's miss would leave a hunter with other chances.

Tamanmo said to the bowman, 'Can you send a flaming arrow onto the roof of that store?'

The bowman said, 'Yes, Tamanmo. I came prepared, just in case such was needed.'

'Do it then,' Tamanmo said.

He watched as the brave withdrew dried moss from his quiver, squeezed pine pitch from a pouch to fasten it just behind the arrowhead, and notched the arrow in his bow. He drew the bow only until it was near the combustible wad.

A brave, with flint-and-steel, ignited the wad, and the bowman released the missile.

It arced true and struck the weather-dried shake roof.

In moments, the roof burst into flames.

*　　*　　*

In the store, it was a while before they knew it. They only wondered that the Indians had stopped shooting from across the street.

Then the heat made them aware, followed by a burning shake that landed at their feet.

Seaver stomped it out.

Another embered fragment fell, landing in Ella's hair.

Seaver knocked it free, feeling the scorch of it against his hand.

'You've got to get out of here,' he said. 'The place is on fire!'

'But there's no rear door,' she said. 'Only the side door we came in earlier.'

'Use it,' he said. 'Get out. I'll give a covering fire to keep the Indians busy. Get out and get shelter somewhere else.'

'And you?'

'I'll follow, once you're safe.'

A sudden shower of sparks descended around her, and he gave her a shove. 'Now!' he said.

He returned to a front window and began shooting.

She acted then, running toward the rear through a fall of embers, finally reaching the service door at the side.

Large chunks of burning shakes were dropping now. One struck her shoulder. Panicked, she burst outside.

She was surprised that no enemy shots sought her.

Then a pair of strong brown arms grabbed her, knocking free the rifle she still carried. A moment later she felt herself hoisted on a muscular shoulder and carried rapidly away toward the store structure's front.

Straight toward where the enemy was now meeting Seaver's fire.

As she was carried across the street, struggling against the grasp on her legs, she raised her head and saw that Seaver's weapon, shoved out the window, was not belching smoke.

Was he wounded? Dead? Or just afraid of hitting her if he fired?

She could not know. She did know she was being carried by an Indian.

She was dumped hard onto the ground. So hard that she was stunned. When she recovered, moments later, she was looking at buckskinned legs and moccasins, and heard a man's voice speaking in a native tongue she could not understand.

He seemed to be expressing satisfaction before abruptly giving what sounded like an order.

She was grabbed by the arm and jerked to her feet amid a bunch of staring Sheepeaters.

They began moving away in the direction from which they had charged earlier. They pushed her along with them roughly after she instinctively balked.

*   *   *

Seaver, not daring to shoot for fear of hitting her, watched her being carried across and into the Indian concealment.

He thought, What can I do now?

And at that moment the burning roof started collapsing around him.

He took his chances, and burst out the front door, barely clearing the portico as it fell.

A single burst of rifle fire ripped into the flaming timber beside him. He raced around the north side of the burning structure.

As he reached the lane behind the building, Dorsey suddenly appeared and stopped him.

Dorsey said anxiously, 'Did Ella get out of there?'

Seaver said, 'She got out, ahead of me. Got out and got taken by the Indians.'

'You let that happen?'

'When I saw it, a buck was running with her on his shoulder. I couldn't risk a shot.'

'What now?' Dorsey said.

'We've got to get her back!'

'The Indians have stopped shooting.' Dorsey said. 'Why?'

'Who knows?' Seaver said. 'But maybe they got what they wanted—Ella. Catch up your horse. We got to get mounted and go after them.'

He ran toward where they'd picketed the horses. He threw a saddle on his and fought to get it bridled.

Dorsey was doing likewise.

Both mounts were acting up, nervous from all the shooting.

By the time he hauled up into the seat, Seaver was swearing steadily. He kicked the mount into a run and headed out of town.

Dorsey was right behind him.

They reached the end of the street and found it blocked by a line of armed miners, several holding shotguns.

The big miner, Bearcat, was in the center of the line.

He raised the barrel of a Greener. He looked mean enough to use it.

The threat of the shotgun was too much to ignore. Seaver slid his mount to a halt.

Dorsey just missed colliding with him.

'Running off?' Bearcat said. 'Now that the store is gone and our season's supplies are burned up?'

Seaver said, 'Stand aside! They've taken the woman.'

'The hell with her!' Bearcat said. 'The whole bunch of you ought to be given to the Injuns.'

'They burned the store,' Dorsey said. 'Not us.'

'You're the ones that brought it on,' another said. Seaver glanced his way and saw it was Kelly.

135

'Sorry it happened,' Seaver said.

'What the hell difference does that make to me?' Kelly said. 'I'm out of business. Everything I owned. And these men are going to suffer because of it. You've destroyed this camp, is what you bastards have done.'

'And for that you got to pay,' Bearcat said.

Dorsey cut in. 'How much?' he said.

'More than you got,' Kelly said.

'How much?' Dorsey said again.

'You got three thousand dollars?'

Dorsey was silent, seeming to have an inner struggle. Then he said, 'No.'

'I say lynch them,' Bearcat said.

There was a short chorus of assent from the other miners.

'Hang the bastards high,' one of them said.

Kelly frowned, but made no comment.

Off to one side Seaver saw Bunce and Griffin sitting on the ground. Both were trussed, hand and foot.

Bunce said, 'Me and Griff here was just taking orders. None of this was our wanting.' He paused, then said, 'Dorsey is an ex-army officer. Seaver was a army scout. Fighting Injuns was their business, not ours.'

'Shut up!' Griffin said.

Bunce looked regretful. 'Yeah,' he said. 'I shouldn't have said that.'

Kelly said, 'Our quarrel ain't with you boys. I figured who was in charge from the beginning.'

136

Seaver said, 'Kelly, you met the woman. You know what the Indians will likely do to her?'

Kelly was silent.

'You want that to happen?'

'Of course not,' Kelly said. 'But I figure it's too late to stop it.'

'I don't,' Seaver said. 'But time is wasting while you hold us here.'

He kept his eyes on Kelly because he could see a struggle going on in the man. 'Well?'

Before Kelly could answer, Bearcat said, 'Don't listen to him, Kelly. And it ain't for you to say. It's us that's going to suffer for these bastards bringing their Injun trouble onto us. The hell with the woman!'

'No!' Kelly said.

'What the hell you mean—no?'

'What I said. Listen to me, all of you—you need supplies brought in here to keep you going? Then I'm the only one can get them for you. I got the contacts that can get replacements packed in. So you'll have to live off the country for a few weeks. But I'll set up a new store somehow.' He paused. 'But only if you free these men to go after the woman.'

Bearcat said, 'By God! Kelly you must have been some took by that wench.'

Kelly said angrily, 'She isn't a wench. She's a lady.'

'Traveling with these hard cases?' Bearcat said. 'Bull!'

137

'You'll believe what you want,' Kelly said. 'You been a woman hater ever since your wife ran off with another man years ago.'

'A damn good reason, ain't it?' Bearcat grumbled.

Kelly faced the others. He had a fair eye for judging men.

He said, 'Put it to a vote, I say. But if you want me to work to get stuff packed in, you'll vote my way.'

When nobody spoke, he said, 'Well, what's it to be?'

One of them said, 'Don't look like we got much choice, we want to keep on mining.'

'I'll second that,' another said.

From down the line came a majority of assents.

Kelly said, 'Bearcat, put down that Greener. The vote is cast.'

'I don't like it none,' Bearcat said, but he lowered his shotgun.

'All right,' Kelly said to Seaver.

'We won't forget you for this,' Seaver said as he and Dorsey started forward.

'I wish to hell I could forget *you*,' the store owner said.

*　　*　　*

The trail of the Indians was wide open. It was as if they didn't care if they were followed.

Dorsey commented on this.

'Why not?' Seaver said. 'They'll have a rear guard watching for us and an ambush ready if we're spotted.'

'You got a plan to avoid that?'

'No,' Seaver said, and fell into silence.

After a few moments of this, Dorsey said, 'Ella seems to have had a way on that storekeep.'

'Lucky for us.'

'Got a grip on you too, Seaver.'

'Yeah. Kind of grown on you also, I'd say.'

'Something women are born with,' Dorsey said.

'We got to get her back fast,' Seaver said. 'They took her because she shot that one in the face to save me, back there on the mountain.'

'I saw him here,' Dorsey said. 'Looked like he had an eyeball missing.'

'That's what scares me most of all,' Seaver said. 'Indians ain't much different than whites when it comes to taking an eye for an eye.'

'You think they'd blind her?'

'That,' Seaver said, 'might just be the beginning.'

'God!'

'Yeah,' Seaver said. 'My thinking exactly.'

*　　*　　*

They came to the vicinity of where the Indians had halted. Some sixth sense warned Seaver, and he slowed Dorsey. Together they made a

139

wary approach until they sighted the dismounted braves in a clearing surrounded by timber.

They halted to study the gathering.

'Braves only,' Dorsey said. 'Just the raiding party. Must have left their squaws farther back when they set out last night.'

'The braves and Ella,' Seaver said.

They could see her now.

She was not bound, but was slumped on the ground as if thrown there by an angry brave.

'They're not torturing her, at least,' Dorsey said.

'Not yet,' Seaver said. 'Not until they reach the camp where the squaws are. They'll have the squaws do that. While they watch.'

'We've got to get her,' Dorsey said.

There was a frantic tone to his words, uncharacteristic of the man, Seaver thought. He knew then that Dorsey's feeling toward Ella was akin to his own.

'How the hell do we get her?' Dorsey said.

*   *   *

Tamanmo had called the halt.

Some of his braves, including two wounded, showed concern at his order.

One of them even protested, saying, 'We may be pursued.'

Tamanmo ignored the protest. 'Pull the woman off the horse,' he said.

140

The brave obeyed, then flung her to the ground.

'I will have some of my revenge now,' Tamanmo said.

The protesting brave said, 'It is something best left for our females to do. When we have distanced ourselves from any pursuit and can fully enjoy watching.'

'We will briefly rest the horses,' Tamanmo said, 'and amuse ourselves while we do so. I thirst for a taste of what is to come.'

He walked over then and kicked her.

He said, 'First I will put out her eye, as she has done to me.'

There was a muttering of approval from the braves.

'Bind her so she cannot move,' Tamanmo said.

A couple of braves went toward her with rawhide thongs.

It was obvious she did not understand what had been said, because only at the last did she try futilely to scramble away from them.

They quickly overpowered her and trussed her hand and foot.

Tamanmo stared down at her with his unblinded eye.

'Get me a pointed stick,' he said.

The brave who wore the quiver, and who had started the fire at the store, drew an arrow loose, and held it up.

'Will this do better, Tamanmo?' he said.

141

Tamanmo took it and fondled the point.

'It will do fine,' he said.

He reached out then, and held the point in front of Ella's right eye.

CHAPTER THIRTEEN

'Christ!' Dorsey said.

Seaver raised his rifle.

'Three hundred yards,' Dorsey said. 'At least.'

Ella's back was toward them. The Indian was facing her, and it was obvious to them what he was going to do.

At that distance Seaver could not draw a bead on him without possibly putting a bullet into Ella's back.

Rifle to cheek, he hesitated.

Dorsey said, 'Good God, man, don't even think it!'

Seaver knew he was right. There was a time in years past when he might have risked it, but not now.

Instead, he swung the sights to the side, before he raised the barrel and fired.

His high-trajectory shot hit one of the other Indians, who dropped to the ground with a yell.

The one with the arrow ran for cover with the rest of them, including the one Seaver had hit.

Leaving Ella where she was.

'Keep firing,' Seaver said. 'But aim wide of Ella.'

Dorsey grunted, and began blasting away.

The Indians reached their horses, began to mount and flee.

All but the one who had held the arrow in threat.

He made a move as if to return for her.

A shot by Seaver that nicked his horse, causing it to rear and start to break away, changed his action. He caught the rein, fought the animal, managed to mount, and went running after the others.

Dorsey said, 'Lucky you spooked him.'

'Been luckier if I'd hit him,' Seaver said. He moved to his horse, swung up, and said, 'Keep firing.'

'At this distance it won't do any good,' Dorsey said. He stepped to his own horse and mounted. 'We'll do this together.'

They slipped their rifles into scabbards, drew six-guns, and kicked the horses into a run.

They held their fire until a couple of Indians, who had turned, shot aimlessly in their direction.

They shot back, and the Indians retreated.

Seaver and Dorsey reached Ella. Seaver swung down, slashed her bonds, remounted, and pulled her up behind his cantle.

A second later she had both arms wrapped

tight around his waist, clinging for her life.

They pivoted their mounts.

The Indians must have lost their panic, seeing only two attackers, for at that moment their rifle fire began kicking up dirt around the horses' hooves.

It continued even as the riders raced out of range.

They kept riding, only occasionally looking back.

There was no sign of pursuit.

'Our horses have been resting these past few days,' Seaver said. 'Theirs haven't.'

'You think we've seen the last of them?'

'Not at all,' Seaver said.

Ella's arms around him had loosened their grasp. 'Oh God!' she said. 'Won't they ever give up?'

'They have a debt to collect.'

'For the girl Sandow killed,' Ella said. 'But his life was taken in turn.'

'But not by them,' Seaver said. 'That makes the difference.'

'But now it's more than that,' she said. 'That Indian chief apparently blames me for his disfigurement. I could tell his eye is blinded and I think he meant to blind me!'

'He may quit now, ma'am,' Dorsey said. 'He may tire of the chase.'

She was silent, then said to Seaver, 'Might he?'

'Not likely,' Seaver said.

Dorsey turned in his saddle and gave him a cold stare. 'Did you have to tell her that?'

'It's what I think.'

'You don't know much about women's feelings, do you?'

'It didn't seem right to lie,' Seaver said.

Ella seemed to sense the conflict between them. She said, 'I owe my sight, and my life, to both of you.'

'For you, ma'am,' Dorsey said, 'I would do it anytime.'

'Thank you, Mr Dorsey.'

Her words gave Seaver a moment of jealousy.

Then he felt her arms around him tighten in a quick squeeze and hold there, and pleasure took its place.

*　　*　　*

They reached the diggings and found Kelly and some of the miners surveying the burnt debris of his store. Some of the log walls remained.

At their approach, the miners looked up, and anger immediately showed on the faces of most.

Only Kelly showed relief. 'God,' he said, 'I'm glad you got her back.'

The big miner, Bearcat, was there, and said, 'Get out of town, Seaver.'

'That's our plan.'

'Now!'

The sooner, the better, Seaver was thinking. Not because of the miner's threat, but because of the Indians.

That seemed to be Bearcat's motive too. 'Them Injuns come back now, they'll be madder than a hornet. And we don't need no more tussle with them. Been enough damage done already.'

'Soon as we pick up my two men,' Dorsey said.

Kelly nodded toward the bivouac area. 'They're loafing over yonder.'

'We'll be on our way then,' Seaver said. 'We get out, we'll pass the word that you'll be needing supplies real bad.'

'Do that,' Kelly said. 'But I'll be leaving in a day or two, myself.'

'You could go with us,' Seaver said.

'I got to take stock of what I need first. And, by God, I don't want them Injuns thinking I'm one of you.'

'I understand,' Seaver said.

'Best of luck with the lady,' Kelly said. 'I hope you can get her out safe.' He paused. 'It's only because of that hope that you two missed getting lynched.'

Dorsey's face hardened. There was still enough officer in him to resent being so addressed. Or perhaps it was the hardcase in him now. But he refrained from lashing back, although Seaver could see the effort it cost him.

Seaver took Kelly's comment as probably

146

deserved. He realized that staging the Indian standoff in Kelly's town had cost the man, and he felt regret for it.

But what was done, was done, and they had gained little from it; there was danger ahead to contend with.

He had better be thinking about that, not dwelling on a past mistake. He had gambled on ending the Indian trouble with the miners' help. Gambled and lost. And that was that.

Dorsey seemed not to share Seaver's regret for what had been done, or perhaps it was his resentment at Kelly's tall tones that made him ask, 'What about some foodstuff for us? We got a way to go yet.'

'You got balls to ask that?' Kelly said. 'Eat game like these miners will have to do.' He paused. 'And get the hell out of my town! Now!'

He seemed to remember Ella then. His face flushed with embarrassment.

'Pardon my dirty language, ma'am,' he said. 'And I'll give you what I can spare.'

*   *   *

Kelly had done them one last favor. He pointed out the pack trail he used to the outside.

Seaver nodded his thanks, and now led the way on it.

'It's tough going,' Kelly had said. 'But if

them Injuns don't catch up to you again, you ought to get out in a week at the latest.'

Seaver wasn't so sure. Kelly had sent them off without adequate provisions, and for the first time they had trouble finding any game. By the second day hunger was with them, and Seaver called a halt while they spread out to hunt. They came back empty-handed. That night they went to their blankets mealless.

Hoping that up ahead their luck would change, they pushed on.

Ella rode listlessly. Traumatized by her recent experiences, and now beset by hunger, she looked pale and drawn. She made no complaint, in fact spoke almost not at all, and that worried him. It was something that caused both Seaver and Dorsey much thought.

Once, Dorsey said to him, 'Woman like that could cause a man to give up bank robbing.'

It bothered Seaver that his tone was serious.

It also brought back to his mind what he'd learned about the loot Dorsey and his cohorts had taken at Salmon City. The men had apparently split it into their shares, but only Dorsey had flashed any of it around. Seaver had assumed each carried his share hidden in a saddlebag somewhere.

For all of Dorsey's professed love of money, he had been openhanded with it at Kelly's place, Seaver thought. He assumed Dorsey carried more cash than was in his wallet. The man had to be wearing a money belt.

By chance, Seaver walked up when Dorsey was replenishing the money he had spent.

Dorsey was startled, but seeing Seaver's scrutiny on him, made the best of it. He said, 'Want to see it?'

'A money belt?'

Dorsey held the belt out to show it. It was a fine piece of workmanship, of which Dorsey seemed proud. 'I got it from a French Canuck up Fort Benton way. Sealskin, I think. Word he gave me was some of those French boatmen have them, designed to be waterproof.'

'Nice-looking thing,' Seaver had said.

He'd wondered how much currency the belt contained, but it wasn't the kind of question you'd ask.

CHAPTER FOURTEEN

Chris Carter had almost revealed his hand, back there where the Sheepeater chief threatened the white woman. But the shots fired by Seaver and Bart Dorsey had come just in time to prevent his own action.

He was glad, because his whole plan continued to be one of remaining hid until his chance came for him to take Dorsey—and his cohorts too, if possible.

There was also Seaver to think about, a man whose exact relationship with Dorsey was

149

unknown to Carter. Dorsey had once been an army officer, and might well be an old acquaintance of the Indian fighter, and who knew what debts might be owed between them.

If so, together, they made a big handful for a lone bounty hunter to handle.

Now, watching them abruptly leave the mining camp, he saw a possibility of gaining some answers to his questions. He decided to reveal himself to the men of the diggings.

As he rode in, alert and curious, he encountered first the proprietor of the burned store, who was standing by, staring at it.

Carter's eyes fell onto the charred remains of a sign reading *Kelly's*.

'You Kelly?'

Kelly studied him, then nodded.

'I seen some folks ride off like they was in a hurry, back a bit.'

'I run the bastards out of town,' Kelly said, bitterness returning to his voice. 'Hadn't been for them stopping here, them Sheepeaters wouldn't have bothered us. And I'd still have my store.'

'Been a long time since the Sheepeaters caused trouble,' Carter said. 'I remember how it was then, though.'

Kelly's interest rose.

'You have a part in them old doings?'

'Yep. Army guide. For Captain Bernard's cavalry detachment. Back in seventy-nine.'

'Hell, I was one of them. Private Kelly.'

'Chris Carter,' Carter said.

'Carter! Hell, I remember! But, man, you done aged some.'

'Ain't we all?' Carter said.

Kelly moved toward the rider and held out his hand; Carter shook it.

'Light and rest your butt,' Kelly said.

Carter swung down and tied his mount to a still-standing remnant of the hitchrack. 'How well you know them folks who went through?'

'Better than I wanted to. You got a particular interest in them?'

'Might be. Have to know more about them to know for sure.'

Kelly seemed about to speak, then was suddenly silent.

Carter sensed this and said, 'You sound like you weren't too fond of them.'

Kelly hesitated, then said, 'That's a true fact. All except a lady they was escorting. I never did find out what she was doing with that bunch of hard cases.'

'The lady was kidnapped by a renegade Shoshone,' Carter said. 'He got hisself killed a ways back on the trail.'

'Kidnapped by a Injun? Who is she?'

'Might be you've heard of her. A famous lady. Name of Ella Gordon. Writer and lecturer for Injun rights.'

'I never heard of her. But, by God, I knowed she had class. But ain't that a come-all, her being for Injun rights and then getting

151

kidnapped by one of them.'

'Yeah, ain't it so?'

'Wasn't for her,' Kelly said, 'those with her might have stretched some hemp for bringing the Injuns down on us. One man appeared different, was closest to her. Name of Seaver.'

Carter said, 'He just lost an election for sheriff down Silver City way, I heard.'

'He didn't strike me as a lawman type.'

'Army scout,' Carter said. 'Injun fighter. *Jon* Seaver.'

'Seaver? Hell, I heard of him in the old days. Never dawned on me it was *that* Seaver.'

'He'd been kind of forgotten till he showed up to run for office,' Carter said.

'We don't get much news in here, months at a time.'

Carter nodded. 'Ain't much different than it was in the old days.'

'For a fact,' Kelly said. 'These last few days especially.' He paused. 'So what's your interest in the bunch went through?'

'Seaver and the woman, not much. They got mixed up with the others by accident. Seaver come in here, I guess, tracking her and the Injun that stole her.'

'And the others?'

'Robbed the bank at Salmon City. I'm what's left of the posse that set out after them. By description, it's Bart Dorsey and a couple of his men.'

'Dorsey was his name, all right. Bank

152

robber, you say? No wonder he had some money.' Kelly stopped suddenly, then said, 'By God, he probably had enough loot to replace my losses here, had I only knowed!'

Carter said, 'No doubt. The posse left Salmon in a hurry, but the rumor was his take was several thousand.'

'Damn!' Kelly said. 'And a bounty on his head, too, no doubt?'

'That's why I'm here. Been tracking him for days now.'

'Well, they ain't far ahead.'

'They ain't ever been far ahead,' Carter said. 'The trick is to take them without getting killed.'

'Well, I hope you get the bastard.'

'I'll get him,' Carter said. 'Sooner or later.'

'Don't be too sure,' Kelly said. 'We had enough men here to drive off a Sheepeater attack, but them Injuns got a score of some kind to settle with that traveling bunch. And they just may beat you to it.'

Chris Carter said, 'I don't intend to let that happen.'

He took to the Dorsey bunch's trail immediately. He was ahead of the Indians now, and it was his aim to keep it that way. He had been close to getting cheated out of his prey by them a couple of times, and worry about losing his chance at the sizable bounty was always with him.

He had bounty-hunted men before, but

never had he encountered so many complications caused by other parties.

Even the woman was a problem. She was a well-known, influential person, and he would be risking harm to her in any shootout around her. And that could cause reverberations.

*   *   *

As they rode along, Ella came close to Seaver and said, 'I keep thinking about that terrible moment when the one they called Tamanmo held that arrow in front of my face. And yet I could not turn away. Seeing what I had done to him held me transfixed. It was as if I deserved what he was about to do.'

'You have to forget it.'

'I can't.'

Seaver said, 'I don't mean forget what he was about to do to you. Let that teach you what his kind is capable of. I mean you've got to forget what you did to him. You were only acting to save my life.'

'I have told myself that was so.'

'It's true, so believe it.'

'Yes, you are right,' she said. She dropped back a little then, as if she could not bear to discuss it further.

Seaver shook his head in annoyance. The sensitiveness of women was beyond him.

*   *   *

From time to time, Carter had them in sight.

He was taking care to keep a distance that he hoped would hide his own presence. He knew they would be on the lookout for resumption of pursuit by the Sheepeaters. That made him doubly careful.

He also cast frequent looks behind him. In the mood the Indians seemed to be in, any lone white man could be a target.

The thought occurred to him then that once he had Dorsey in hand, both could become victims of the aroused Sheepeaters.

He let go with a string of curses. Had he foreseen the problems that would confront his quest, he would have dropped out with the rest of the posse when they had reached the Primitive Area.

Still, there was a thousand-dollar bounty on Dorsey's head, and he had come too far to give up until he had his man.

He had to figure a way to accomplish this, get out of the Sheepeater area with his captive, and head for the nearest town that had a sheriff, so as to put in his claim for the reward.

And he had to do it soon.

*   *   *

Tamanmo was angered.

The bold attack had panicked his braves, himself included, and lost him his woman captive. His frustration was sharpened by the

155

abrupt halt to that moment of climax he would have savored by thrusting his arrow into her eye.

Since he would not give vent to anger at himself, he turned upon the slightly wounded young brave who had cried out as the attackers' bullet gouged his leg. Tamanmo now blamed that for starting the rout of his men.

The other braves seemed ready enough to agree.

'A warrior does not yelp at a wound of the flesh,' Tamanmo said to the youth. 'He does not behave like a dog hit by a thrown stone.'

The brave was not yet out of his teens, and this rebuke pained him worse than the minor wound.

He said, 'It will not happen again, Tamanmo.'

Tamanmo accepted that grudgingly.

An older brave said, 'Will we now give up this chase? Our women are mostly unprotected. The few men we left at the camp are not enough. They are not even the best of hunters.'

'We will go on,' Tamanmo said.

'But twice now we have tried and failed,' the brave said.

'We will go on until we succeed.'

'But our women—'

'We will go on,' Tamanmo said again.

Ever since they had together rescued Ella, something had changed between Seaver and Dorsey.

Each had put his life on the line for her, and out of that had grown something that made them rivals.

Seaver's realization of this grew as they rode along the pack trail, separated by a few yards from each other, and from her. He was leading the way when uneasiness drove him to glance backward beyond Ella to where Dorsey rode, straight in his saddle as always.

Their glances met, and he could see the change in Dorsey's eyes.

He let his glance sweep toward Ella and found her own stare upon him, her expression curious, yet knowing. Yes, he thought, she feels it, too.

His own face turned grim as he twisted forward again, aware that what had occurred here could mean trouble ahead.

Trouble on top of trouble, he was thinking.

And that was something he didn't need.

* * *

Since Kelly, after first refusing to sell them any salvaged provisions, had relented only to furnish them bare rations for a day's travel, and that only because of Ella's presence,

Seaver felt the urgent need to find game, and find it soon.

Previously game had been available when needed, mule deer especially. But now they went into the third day without sight of any.

Their hunger grew.

And both Seaver and Dorsey kept casting concerned glances at Ella.

She had been through a lot recently for a woman of her background, Seaver thought. And the fact she did not complain impressed him, as it seemed to impress Dorsey.

Even Bunce and Griffin, who earlier had ignored her after their initial male interest in her had been dampened by Dorsey's restrictive orders, now looked at her often, but with concern rather than desire.

But they were all hungry, and tempers grew short.

It seemed to Seaver that this was particularly true between himself and Dorsey.

Where before they had gotten along without friction, possibly because each had a background of army service that involved a measure of respect for the professional expertise of the other's calling, they now bridled at each other.

The testiness seemed to wane when, on the third afternoon, Seaver startled a bull elk and shot it on the run.

They stopped right there to butcher and roast and feast on it.

The testiness waned, but it did not vanish entirely.

*　　*　　*

Chris Carter, following them, but woodsman enough to avoid disclosing his presence to them, was constantly in a state of fret.

Twice he had spotted the distant smoke from what he judged were the Sheepeaters cook fires no more than a half a day behind him.

They were gaining on him and on those he pursued. It was coming down to a matter of time, he thought.

He had been weighing his options, and although fearful the Indians might cheat him out of his prey, he could not see his way clear to ride into the whites' camp and try to make an arrest.

Besides Dorsey himself, there were his two hardcase gunhands, and these odds were, to Chris, too much for a man of his age. There had been a time when he would have gone in and taken his chances. But his reflexes were not what they had been, and he knew it.

Then, too, there was the unknown quantity of Jon Seaver he would have to reckon with.

Seaver might side with him, or he might side with Dorsey. But, from Carter's observation thus far, the two appeared to work well enough together. This bothered him greatly.

Enough that he was of a mind to gamble that

159

the whites would escape from the wilderness area before the Indians could catch up and attack them again.

There, outside in the open country beyond what the Sheepeaters considered their habitat, the Indians might abandon their pursuit.

If so, he decided, that would be the place to make his move.

*   *   *

One of Tamanmo's braves returned from a scout, and said, 'There is another white man following the whites. He has somehow got between us and them.'

'What does he look like?' Tamanmo asked. 'Is he armed? Does he look like a warrior?'

'He has a rifle and a handgun, and he is watching the others without revealing himself.'

Tamanmo thought about this, then said. 'Does he wear a star of metal on his chest?'

'A star of metal?' the brave said.

Tamanmo said, 'Once I was in the white mans' place called Salmon City. I learned something from one of our people who lived there. Among the whites, there are a few who wear a metal star. They do so to keep the others from crimes against each other.'

The brave looked puzzled, as if he found this hard to believe. But, after a pause, he said, 'I did not see any such star.'

Tamanmo considered this in silence, then he

160

said, 'It makes no difference. If he hides from those he follows, he must be an enemy of them. And if this is so, he could, for reasons of his own, interfere in my plan for our coming attack.'

'So what do we do?' the brave said.

'I will send you to take him captive,' Tamanmo said to the scout. 'And we will make him tell what he is doing. Take five braves and go.'

*   *   *

Carter had seen the Indian scout, and now he cursed himself, fearful the Indian had likewise seen him.

He had been careful, keeping to the north flank of the traveling whites, knowing the Sheepeaters were closing in.

The latter fact had possibly upset his judgment. He had been worrying that the Dorsey party might not escape the wilderness before the Indians struck again. And he had let the Indians get too close.

Knowing he had been seen, he decided to withdraw farther to the north, hoping the redskins would not bother to search for him. They would be intent now on their attack, he told himself.

He only half believed that.

The half-belief did not stay with him, and as he moved northward, he decided to flee the scene altogether.

He could come back later. Maybe.

The thousand-dollar bounty on Dorsey's head was starting to lose its importance to him. A man his age ought to have more sense than to be lured by it. The trouble was, he thought, that with age your common sense seemed to decrease a little.

He had been noticing that more and more lately.

He hastened his pace away from where any search detail of the Sheepeaters should be.

And rode head-on into a half dozen of them who had apparently slipped ahead to ambush him.

They could have killed him then and there. But their leader raised his hand in a sign of peace.

He saw the peace gesture, but he also saw the leveled weapons of the others.

His oldster's mind made a quick decision.

A decision based somewhat on his notice of these Indians' persistent animosity toward the other whites. And, too, there was the hacked-up condition of the hanging corpse, and the near blinding of the white woman captive. It also came from a mindset ever conscious that he had a natural life expectancy nearing its end anyway. So, weighing this against a powerful fear that to surrender might mean unbearable torture, he acted impulsively.

He made a frantic grab at his holstered gun,

drew, and shot the surprised brave who had his hand raised. Carter pivoted his horse and went crashing through the timber's undergrowth.

The startled braves fired their weapons, but he felt no hits.

You crazy old bastard, he thought. *You must have made the right decision.*

But it wasn't over yet. The Indians could easily match his pace through the heavily forested area. His one chance was to break out into the open before they closed in on him again.

He spurred his horse forward, both of them whipped by limbs and branches.

With no sight of the sun to guide him, he had no real idea of his direction, only a vague sense that he was headed southwest.

When the timber thinned he found himself in the mouth of a rising canyon.

And there, a scant hundred yards away, the whites that traveled with Dorsey were looking up at the sound of his crashing into the clear.

Behind him was the noise of the pursuing Sheepeaters.

Acting on impulse again, Carter raced directly toward the now halted whites.

He caught sight of weapons appearing in their hands.

And then he was among them.

The Indians had stopped in the timbered edge and were sending shots after him.

As he reached the whites, Carter shouted,

163

'Get out of range of them trees!'

He was of a mind to keep riding, but his mount, exhausted from beating a way through the forest, slowed among the other horses.

The whites took his advice, and as they rode, they formed an escort of sorts around him.

Of all things, he found himself riding side by side with Bart Dorsey. He threw a glance in Dorsey's direction and caught his stare. He was certain he saw something in Dorsey's face ... suspicion or recognition.

Old Carter began to sweat again.

CHAPTER FIFTEEN

Dorsey halted once they were out of range of the timber-hidden Sheepeaters' fire.

He ordered them into a firing line of their own, and waited to see if the Indians would venture into the open to engage them again.

As he expected, they were not that foolish.

He looked at Carter, who had positioned himself several yards away. 'What happened, old man?' he called.

'What the hell you mean—old man?' Carter yelled back peevishly.

'No offense ...,' Dorsey said. 'Just tell us what happened.'

'That's more like it,' Carter said. He hesitated, then said, 'Name's Carter, Chris
164

Carter. Them bastards tried to ambush me. I killed the one leading them, and got away.'

'You figure they'll make a fight of it now?'

Carter shook his head. 'Wasn't more than five, six of them. They'll want better odds.'

'What are you doing out here?' Dorsey asked. The oldster seemed to have no ready answer, and Dorsey said, 'Well?'

'I come looking to see could I find a white woman was took by a renegade Injun out of Silver City,' Carter said.

'Why?'

'Ain't there a reward to bring her back?'

'You tell me,' Dorsey said.

Carter gestured over to where Ella was positioned behind Seaver. 'Ain't that Ella Gordon?'

'That's her.'

'There's a reward, all right. And that's what brought me into the area here, looking.'

Dorsey eyed him shrewdly, and the old man's own stare dropped.

'If that's your reason, you're a little late. Jon Seaver over there already rescued her.'

'That's Jon Seaver?'

'That's him.'

'Well, then, it looks like I took a hard trail and near got ambushed all for nothing,' Carter said. 'Be no other reason for me to come in here.'

'No?'

'You think of any other reason?' Carter

asked.

'I might.'

'Well,' Carter said. 'I told you the true one. And it looks like it all turned out for nothing.'

Dorsey held a probing stare on him until the old man began to fidget. Then he seemed to relent, and Dorsey said grudgingly, 'All right. You can travel with us. I don't know what else I can do with you, short of shooting you.'

'What the hell you talking about?' Carter said. 'About shooting me?'

'I think you know,' Dorsey said.

Carter started to protest, then stopped.

Dorsey said, 'You shot one of the Indians, you say. Let me tell you that this band of Sheepeaters isn't a forgiving bunch. We've been learning from experience that they never give up their goal of vengeance.' He paused. 'Alone out there now, your chances would be mighty slim.'

'I'm obliged for your concern,' Carter said cautiously. Then he said, 'You ever had much experience with Injuns? I mean before this.'

'I had my share,' Dorsey said. 'But stop playing games, Carter. You know who and what I am.'

On the other side of Dorsey, Bunce and Seaver had been listening and catching parts of the conversation. Now Bunce said in a low voice, 'Listen, Dorsey. Turn the old bastard out and let the Injuns take him. He ain't here looking for the woman. He's here for a bounty

166

on us.'

'I can't do that,' Dorsey said. 'He's a stubborn enough old man to take up where he left off.'

'Keep his guns,' Bunce said.

'Turn him out without arms for defense or hunting?'

'Then shoot him,' Bunce said.

'No way. Could you?'

Bunce did not answer at once. Then he said, 'No, I guess not. Not in cold blood.'

'So we're stuck with him,' Dorsey said. 'But there's an up side to it. He's no doubt a good shot with his rifle, next time the Indians attack.'

'Yeah,' Bunce said. 'Provided he don't turn it against us instead.'

'Not likely, in the company of us all.'

'I wouldn't be too sure,' Bunce said. 'Kind of depends if the bounty reads "Dead or Alive," don't it?'

'I'll keep his arms when we're not in combat,' Dorsey said.

'I still don't like it.'

'Neither do I,' Dorsey said. 'But that's the way it's going to be.'

He turned toward Carter.

'Looks like this standoff is over for now, Chris. You can ride with us, but you've got to surrender your arms.'

'Like hell!' Carter said. 'You just said your own self these Injuns don't quit trying.'

167

'They try again, you'll get your weapons back.'

Carter made no move and said nothing.

'That's an order,' Dorsey said.

'Was a time people trusted me not to turn on my own kind,' the old man said.

'Was a time you weren't bounty hunting, either.'

'Well, the passing years can drive a man to desperation,' Carter said. He moved toward Dorsey, offering his weapons.

Dorsey took them. 'There's truth in what you say.'

They moved on, but the presence of Carter added another tension among them.

Griffin voiced his feeling to Dorsey. 'Bart, as a ex-officer, you ought to have more sense than to let him stay. Send him on his way.'

'Like I said before, it's safer to have him here under watch than out there trailing us.'

'I ain't so sure about that,' Griffin said. 'But there's the other thing. The old man says he shot that brave tried to capture him. That's more cause to keep them Sheepeaters coming.'

When Dorsey did not answer, Griffin turned to Seaver. 'You know Injuns better than most. What's your thought?'

'There's no bounty on me,' Seaver said. 'So I've got no worry about that. But I wouldn't turn him out without a means of defense, not the way the Indians are acting.'

Griffin said, 'If he hadn't been bounty-hunting us, he wouldn't be in trouble. Serves the old son of a bitch right.'

'Even so,' Seaver said.

'Even so, hell!' Griffin said. 'He's another reason for them Injuns to hate our guts.'

'In my way of thinking,' Seaver said, 'one more reason doesn't make much difference.'

'You damn army men all think alike,' Griffin said.

Seaver shot a glance at Dorsey, who stared back.

Then Seaver said, 'No, that's not true. But in this case, I think Dorsey is right.'

'You won't think so if the old coot gets hold of a weapon and starts shooting.' Griffin turned to Dorsey. 'And you'll be his prime target.'

Seaver said, 'I don't think so. Dorsey, I remember seeing a wanted dodger on you in the Silver City sheriff's office. I believe that the reward was a thousand dollars for bringing you in alive, and only half of that for you dead.'

'That don't make sense,' Griffin said.

'It does if you're a banker. And it's a banker group posting the reward. I've seen those terms before. The reason is that from a live prisoner they've got a chance to recover stolen property or learn the locality of hidden loot. From a dead one, which is easier for a bounty hunter, they can learn nothing.'

'I wouldn't trust the old coot to know the difference,' Griffin said. He paused. 'That

169

dodger say anything about me or Bunce?'

'Not that I remember.'

'All right, then,' Griffin said. 'Bart, you're the one taking the big risk.'

The answer from Dorsey was nothing more than a curt nod. It was plain enough that it angered him to have his men question his decisions.

*   *   *

Once again, they moved steadily along. Two more days passed. Even Seaver began to think the Sheepeaters had tired of their unsuccessful pursuit.

Carter seldom spoke to anyone. Several times though, Seaver caught Carter's eyes on him, and saw there what he judged a desire to speak privately, away from Dorsey and his men.

Seaver was aware now that the old mountain man had been tracking Dorsey ever since the Salmon City bank robbery, with thought of reward in mind.

Well into the second day of Carter's presence, Seaver's curiosity caused him to drop back and let Dorsey lead the way.

He pulled alongside Carter, gestured him to slow, until a scowling Bunce and Griffin passed them by. Bunce turned in his saddle, his own curiosity showing, then shrugged and turned back to the trail, ignoring them.

Seaver said then, 'Carter, you been wanting to talk to me?'

The oldster said, 'That I have, Seaver. You and me, I figure, have been pretty much two of a kind. We ain't always been saints, maybe, but we sure as hell ain't of the owlhoot breed like these others.'

'So?'

'And last I heard you just lost a election for sheriff down in Owyhee County.'

'That's right,' Seaver said.

'Kind of makes you next thing to a lawman,' Carter said.

Seaver was silent.

'Like me,' Carter said.

'Like you?'

'Ain't that what a bounty hunter is?'

Seaver said, 'Well, you can get arguments about that.'

'Dammit!' Carter leaned close as he could in his saddle, and said in a low voice, 'You and me together, we could take these three hardcases.'

'What reason would I have to do that?'

'A split of the bounty, that's why.'

Seaver looked up ahead, past Bunce and Griffin, to where Dorsey rode beside Ella. They appeared to be in compatible conversation, and he was irritated by the sight.

He drew his mind back to Carter's proposition.

Carter said, 'You'd be free then of any trouble these owlhoots can make you about the

171

woman. There's a big reward if you take her in, and you know it. But Dorsey may have his own ideas about that.'

That, Seaver thought, had been an increasing worry with him. At the beginning, Dorsey had indicated a plan for sharing the reward.

Now his worry went deeper than that. Dorsey obviously had an amorous interest in Ella, not unlike his own.

What future could the bank robber possibly contemplate with her? he thought.

And then the question came to mind: What kind of a future could *I* have with her?

He had no answer for that.

Carter broke in on his thought.

'Are you hearing what I say, Seaver?'

'I heard.'

'And?'

'It's something I'll give some thought to.'

Seaver was staring ahead as he spoke, and Dorsey, almost as if he'd overheard their conversation, suddenly turned in his saddle to stare back.

Dorsey was no fool. It was likely he would be suspicious of this conference back here.

Thus far he and Dorsey had traveled and fought side by side, out of necessity, but that could all change in a hurry.

Which brought Seaver to think that Carter's suggestion was something to consider. In a way, it was a tempting consideration, but not something he'd be proud of.

Carter said, 'Don't waste too much time thinking. A chance comes, we got to be ready to take it.'

Seaver gave a short nod, gigged his horse, and rode up to where Dorsey was with Ella.

Dorsey said, 'What's the old man talking about?'

Seaver hesitated, then said, 'He's concerned with what you might do with him.'

'I figured that.'

'I might ask that question myself.'

'Nothing,' Dorsey said. 'I'm giving him our protection from the Indians.'

'I think he wonders why.'

'A good question, I suppose. I know his reputation—I heard about his earlier days in the Rockies, and I kind of admire the old man. That influenced my decision.' Dorsey paused. 'Damned foolish maybe on my part, knowing his intentions toward me. But for the time being, I don't see he could be much of a threat. Later, when we're clear of the area, I'll let him go. At his age he isn't likely to resume his tracking.'

'He's a stubborn old cuss,' Seaver said.

'Dammit, Seaver, that's part of what I admire about him.'

'Enough to discount his danger.'

'I'm taking that chance.'

'So you are,' Seaver said.

'Maybe he'll appreciate me giving him

refuge.'

'Maybe,' Seaver said.

Ella was listening intently, and now she said, 'You can be a compassionate man, Mr Dorsey. Surprisingly so.'

Dorsey took that in silence. Then he said, 'It's really more than that, Miss Gordon.' He paused. 'In some ways the old man reminds me of my father.'

She and Seaver both looked at him questioningly.

But Dorsey didn't say any more.

*   *   *

Tamanmo was enraged.

The five men he had sent out with his scout to capture the lone white stranger had just returned bearing the scout's body.

Their account of what had happened infuriated him further.

How could one old man escape from six picked braves? he demanded.

They tried to explain by stressing the part played by the main party of whites.

'Those again!' he shouted.

The braves were shocked at the loss of control he was showing.

This was not the Tamanmo of old, reserved and sagacious for his years. This was a man driven by his frustrations to the borderline of madness.

And yet they awaited his command. Among their people, madness itself earned a strange respect. Madness had sometimes driven earlier warriors to historical deeds of valor.

Some believed that madness could be the expression of spiritual wisdom.

And so they continued to listen when Tamanmo spoke.

When he did so again, his voice had suddenly quieted. It was as if he were repeating a revelation that had been made to him.

'This is what must be done,' he said. 'There is one white man among those others who is leading the way. He is to be stopped. Killed from a distance.'

A brave said, 'And which is he, Tamanmo?'

'He is the one who took the white woman from us, back there near the miners' town.'

'But there were two,' the brave said.

'He is the one who is always closest to the white woman,' Tamanmo said. 'Because he is the one, the Shoshone Pandre said, who came to take her from him.'

'Will you be the one who shoots him, Tamanmo?'

'With a blinded eye?'

'Who, then?'

'Who, besides me, has always been the best shot with a rifle?'

The brave hesitated, then said, 'Me, Tamanmo.'

'So you are chosen. You must get close

175

enough to make your shot sure.'

'And if I am that close, and I kill the one you want, will I kill others?'

'Of course, if you can,' Tamanmo said. 'But first make sure you kill the one who is always close to the white woman.' He stopped suddenly, then said. 'But do not shoot *her*. You understand?'

'I understand,' the brave said.

'Then be on your way.'

*   *   *

Carter managed to get near Seaver again, as they made camp.

'Are you with me or not?' the old man said.

'No.'

'No? No wonder they voted you down for sheriff. Hell of a lawman you'd make, won't even try to arrest a bank robber.'

'I didn't get the badge,' Seaver said. 'So I won't do the work.'

'Hell, man, I said we'd split the bounty.'

'It doesn't weigh out against what Dorsey and I been through together these past few days,' Seaver said.

'He'll make you trouble when it comes to the woman,' Carter said. 'He's been cozying up to her, can't you see that?'

'I see it.'

'Owlhoot like him wants her, he ain't going to let you take her in to get that reward,' Carter said.

'I've considered that,' Seaver said.

'Then you're a pure damn fool not to join me to take him out now.'

'Might be,' Seaver said. 'But that's the way it is.'

*   *   *

Carter awoke in the early morning. He studied what he could see of the sky beyond the pine tops, and judged it was close to dawn.

He carefully moved his head to scrutinize the sleeping forms.

Dorsey had posted Griffin as guard earlier. Carter looked for him and saw he had been replaced by Bunce. Bunce leaned against a tree trunk, holding his rifle, but with his chin down on his chest.

Asleep, Carter thought. He wouldn't be playing possum in that uncomfortable position.

Or would he?

Off to one side of where Bunce was slumped was their collection of saddles.

Carter remembered watching Dorsey place his there, and he recalled taking particular interest at the time. But only now did he realize why he had done so.

This could be my chance, he thought. My handgun is in Dorsey's saddlebag.

The other weapons were lying about close to

177

their sleeping owners.

Well, at this point a rifle would be of no use to him. He couldn't keep it hidden. But if he could recover his revolver, stash it away in his own saddlebag, it could play a key role in any future plan.

He began to crawl toward the saddles. At every yard he paused, waiting to see if Bunce moved. He gained reaching distance of Dorsey's gear, and still Bunce sat with lowered head.

He was sweating now. He could feel the wetness of his palms as he fumbled in Dorsey's bags, searching for the gun.

He found it, drew it out, then shifted toward his own saddle and slipped it into the pouch. He crawled back to his blanket and lay under it, panting from exertion, his eyes fixed on the sleeping figure of Bunce.

These past few minutes he had been fearful that Bunce would awaken. Now, in his old man's mind, he was angered at the soundness of the sentry's slumber.

Damn no-account, he thought. Injuns could sneak up close enough to put a bullet into any one of us.

After the tension of his action, and the thought of the camp being unguarded by the sentry, he did not go back to sleep.

Bunce did awaken, just as first light came.

And just in time so that Dorsey, arising, did not catch him dozing on duty.

Witnessing this, Carter was rankled further. He was mollified, though, by knowing that now, when he climbed into his saddle, he'd have his gun in his possession.

*　　　*　　　*

They saddled up and moved out again, this time with Dorsey leading on the now well-defined trail.

At his request, Ella rode beside him.

She was not reluctant. It was a change from her usual pairing with Seaver, and although she had a growing feeling for Jon, his near presence kept reminding her that because of him she had critically wounded the Sheepeater chief, an act that continued to haunt her.

She found the ex-officer a compatible riding companion, courteous and educated. The knowledge that he now lived by crime disturbed her, but Seaver had said that a military blunder, in which Dorsey had inadvertently massacred a village of peaceful Indians, had eventually led to his fall from grace. Compassion for the outlaw gripped her and would not let go.

When the shot came, it seemed clearly meant for Dorsey. It passed through his low-crowned hat, tearing it from his head, barely skimming his hair.

His first thought was of Ella's danger, and he drove spurs to send his horse away from her side. Fear and anger made him reckless, and he plunged the mount into the scatter of scrub timber and brush from beyond which he judged the rifle shot had come.

There was a rising slope ahead on which the trees grew denser. A likely spot for a rifleman trying for a distant shot, he thought.

He was possibly hidden from the ambusher. Or was the assassin merely waiting for a better shot?

Carter, trailing at the rear with Seaver, broke away in the direction Dorsey had gone, even as Seaver sped ahead to be with Ella.

At Seaver's advice, the others dismounted to lie prone. Ella lay beside him.

When he looked back, Carter had disappeared, and they could hear him crashing his horse through the timber.

Was the old man losing his mind? Seaver thought. He shook his head. Old Carter had a way of thinking that could keep you guessing.

* * *

Unbeknownst to Dorsey, Carter had trailed him into the timber.

He glimpsed Dorsey dismounting, and he did likewise and followed, as Dorsey moved cautiously up a rise to disappear in heavier growth.

Carter half expected another shot to sound, but none came.

180

Was the sniper waiting for a sure thing? he wondered.

Carter watched Dorsey press forward, revolver in hand. From Carter's vantage point a few yards to the left of Dorsey, he too saw the Indian raising his rifle to aim at Dorsey, who appeared unaware of the danger.

There was a moment when Chris debated his own move.

He could lie low, let the Indian kill the hardcase ex-officer, pick up the body afterward, and claim it for half the bounty. But that would mean transporting a stinking corpse the many miles to a law officer's location to put in his claim.

Carter fisted his own six-gun and shot down the brave who was aiming at Dorsey. The Indian fell, but held onto his rifle and swung its barrel to point at Carter.

There was a blend of both weapons firing. The brave caught the revolver bullet in the head, shattering his skull.

Carter took the rifle shot through his heart.

Dorsey moved cautiously to where he could see both bodies lying. He let his eyes linger longest on that of the old man, who had saved his life.

CHAPTER SIXTEEN

They managed to scrape out a shallow grave for Chris Carter.

The body of the Indian sniper they left as he had fallen.

Dorsey said, 'It may make that damned Indian chief know he'd better give up trying.'

'More likely it'll aggravate him further,' Seaver said.

Bunce said, 'I ain't digging no grave for no Injun.'

'Goes for me too,' Griffin said. 'We were damn fools to even help bury the old codger.'

'He saved my life,' Dorsey said. 'I owe him for that.'

'Well, you don't owe the Injun nothing,' Griffin said. 'Let's get to moving.'

'All right. Mount up.' Dorsey swung into his saddle.

This time the trail was wider. They rode three abreast, Ella between Dorsey and Seaver.

The two men kept a strained silence. Only Ella turned her head now and then to look at one or the other. But she kept her thoughts to herself.

She was aware that each felt protective toward her. And that should have given her pleasure. Instead, she was bothered that this had somehow become a source of antagonism between them.

They were men who had lived violent lives, she thought, and she was fearful of where all this would lead. What would happen when, or if, they ever got out of this wild area? It was something she did not want to think about.

*   *   *

Tamanmo awaited the return of the assassin. After a while, he sent another brave to investigate. The brave was gone long enough to put the Sheepeater into an impatient rage.

When the brave finally reported back, Tamanmo did not speak to him. He only stared.

The brave hesitated, fearful to relate the news.

'Have you no tongue?' Tamanmo said, exasperated.

'A white killed him,' the brave said. 'But he killed the white.'

'He did kill the white then?' Tamanmo said, his ire decreasing.

'They killed each other in a duel of guns. He and the old white man.'

'The *old* white man?' Tamanmo's ire came back.

'Yes. I dug up the white's grave to see.'

'What about the white I sent him to kill?'

'It appears that one rode off with the others, unharmed.'

183

Tamanmo's face contorted and the brave instinctively stepped back a pace. There was a long moment while he and the other braves stared at the chief.

Then, once again, Tamanmo's fury seemed to pass, and when he spoke this time, his voice was calm, but hard.

'We will bring up *all* the men of our band. Even the old ones. And any boy able to fire a weapon. Our women will have to remain unguarded. For we will now make all-out war.'

'Leave the women unguarded?' a brave said.

'The enemy is ahead of us,' Tamanmo said 'There is no danger behind.'

Many of those women were the wives and daughters of these braves, and they looked concerned. But none seemed ready to protest.

'We will kill the whites, everyone,' Tamanmo said.

'Even the woman you wanted saved for torture?' one of them said.

'Her too. We will kill them all, any way we can,' Tamanmo said.

*   *   *

The silence was weighing on Ella. Finally she spoke to Dorsey.

'Mr Dorsey, you mentioned the possibility the Indians might cease their efforts against us?'

'That's my hope, ma'am. It has been my

184

experience that they do not usually persist in an attack when they are losing.'

Seaver was silent.

She turned to look at him, and saw he rode with his face set, and his eyes straight forward.

It was obvious he did not agree.

She wanted to believe the ex-officer. Unfortunately, she thought the former Indian fighter knew best. When she met Seaver in Silver City he had tried to explain how easily things got out of hand during warfare with Indians. Regardless of what had caused hostilities, the violence could spill over to hurt the innocent as well as the guilty.

She wished now she had been more receptive to his point of view. She would never have imagined then that she herself would have taken arms against the very people she had spent her career protecting.

Unwillingly, her wounding of the Indian chief had resulted in continuing carnage. Carnage that Seaver believed had not yet ended.

And so they rode that day and the next, slowed now as their horses reached near-exhaustion from ascending and descending in the tortuous terrain. Slowed too, as Seaver had taken to scanning their surroundings for a possible ambush.

She wished they could hurry. She felt it was a race they could well lose, if they failed to reach the end of the wilderness before being overtaken by their stubborn pursuers.

The Indian ponies were accustomed to living off what native pasturage they could get, whereas their own mounts were used to getting supplementary rations of grain. And they carried heavier loads. Weighty saddles, and mostly larger men.

These were the mental torments that were often with her, though she tried hard to shove them away.

Ella looked at Seaver. There was no emotion showing, only features grimly set.

She looked at Dorsey and saw the same.

Despite their differences, she thought, they were in some ways two of a kind.

Then Tamanmo struck.

*　　　*　　　*

The first shot came from behind, and for a moment Seaver thought it was a warning shot fired by Bunce, who had been put on rear guard a few yards back.

But almost at once there was a burst of heavy firing. It was followed by silence.

Griffin yelled, 'They got Bunce!'

Dorsey said, 'This is a poor place to make a stand.'

Seaver said, 'Make a run for it. There's higher ground ahead.'

They kicked their tired mounts into a run. All except Bunce.

It was scary going. The pine growth here was not dense, but it was heavy enough to cut their visibility to a scant few yards.

Seaver had spurred into the lead for this reason. If there were pitfalls ahead he felt driven to be the first to meet them. He trusted himself more than he did Dorsey for this. He turned briefly to see Dorsey urging Ella ahead, staying defensively in back. Griffin was with him, a horse length behind.

The trail was beginning to climb, and Seaver hoped for height and some openness. Assuming there were several attackers, they could not make a stand in a forest; they would be quickly surrounded.

In more open country they could at least see what they were fighting against.

It was the damn Sheepeaters again, of course.

And although Seaver had judged by their past actions that they would not be giving up, he was nevertheless a little surprised at their tenacity.

Dorsey was right when he told Ella that Indians were not inclined to keep up a fight when they were taking losses.

But Seaver, in all his years of Indian fighting, had never knowingly been pitted against a foe who was on a personal vendetta.

How many warriors could the Sheepeater chief have? He had taken several casualties. Was he getting reinforcements? If so, from where?

Dorsey called up to Seaver, 'What do you see ahead?'

'Some height, but still trees,' he called back.

Dorsey must have heard him, because he didn't repeat the question. They were making considerable noise.

Enough so that Seaver couldn't hear if the Indians were close to them or not. But it was no time to stop and listen.

Then abruptly he broke out into the clear.

Ahead was a rising shoulder that also sloped down toward the north.

If they could reach the rolling top, they could drop behind the crest and, lying prone for cover, pick off the oncoming attackers.

As they rode out of the trees, their own sound lessened enough for Seaver to hear their pursuers, not more than a hundred yards behind.

He shouted an order, 'Keep running,' and led the pace.

They were a couple of hundred yards into the open when the Indians reached the clearing. Almost at once the bullets began to fly.

Seaver could hear the firing, but the shots were falling short.

They had to hold their lead until they climbed the shoulder, he thought.

He veered toward his right where the down slope lessened the climb, but only slightly. He wanted height when he took position.

It would be the only advantage they would have. But the horses were slowing on the grade.

The Indians, still on flatter ground, kept running their mounts, pulling closer. The bullets started zinging past. Only the difficulty of aiming from horseback kept them from scoring hits.

Seaver twisted in his saddle and looked back, and saw that Griffin, bringing up the rear, was doing likewise. Griffin was raising his rifle to let go a couple of fast shots by way of discouragement. It didn't work. From his jostling mount his shots went wild, and Griffin turned to face forward again, cursing.

The Indians kept firing, but their aim was no better.

Now the whites were urging their faltering mounts up the final yards of the climb.

They went up and over the low summit, and with surprising luck, found an outcrop of eroded rock close by.

'Dismount!' Seaver yelled.

As they swung down, he said to Ella, 'You'll have to hold the horses. Can you do it?'

Without waiting for an answer he thrust his reins into her hands.

Dorsey and Griffin did likewise.

The blowing, frothing mounts were almost impossible to control. Seaver glimpsed her struggling as the horses milled around, tugging her this way and that. He could only hope they didn't break away from her.

Seaver ran forward to throw himself prone behind a lip of rock, facing the enemy. Dorsey and Griffin were on either side, and they fired in near unison.

Seaver shot a brave off his mount. Dorsey or Griffin hit a charging horse, throwing the rider.

The Indians pivoted to flee as the thrown brave leaped up behind a companion.

The attackers raced away out of rifle range.

Seaver glanced back at Ella. Two of the horses had pulled their reins loose from her hands and had trotted off a few paces. And the others were giving her trouble.

'Griffin,' he said, 'give Ella a hand.'

Griffin looked to see the problem, then slipped back to help.

Seaver turned to study the slope.

The Indians had disappeared.

Dorsey said, 'They went into that brushy draw there to the left.'

Seaver searched out the barely visible cut. In the heat of their run he had paid little note to it. Now he judged it was deeper than he'd thought.

It meant they now had to worry about attack from the upper reaches of that ravine.

It meant the Indians could be working their way up for a flank attack.

Seaver's first thought was to cross back over the skyline to the sloping grade they had just ascended. That possibility ended as a couple of shots came out of the draw, angling upward at them from that side.

Moments later a fusillade came from farther up the draw, striking close and whining in ricochet off the outcrop against which they were now pinned and vulnerable.

Dorsey said, 'What now?'

'Up the shoulder!' Seaver said.

He rushed for the horses, now held under control by Griffin and Ella.

She held the reins of his mount and her own. He boosted her into her saddle, swung into his own, grabbed her reins, and spurred up the slope, leading her.

Behind him, Dorsey and Griffin kicked their mounts to follow.

There was another outcrop ahead, and Seaver drove around and behind it, hearing the splat of bullets as they hit it.

They huddled there, holding their horses.

'Will they never quit?' Ella cried.

Nobody answered her.

Now shots began to come from higher on the shoulder above them.

'How the hell did some of them get up there?' Griffin said.

Dorsey said, 'See the way the escarpment rolls? There's a ravine on that side too, I'd guess.'

Griffin said, 'You were leading the way, Seaver.'

Ella spoke up sharply. 'He had no time to

study terrain! You ought to know that.'

The shooters above now had the range. Bullets were slapping around them.

'Let's charge the bastards,' Griffin said.

'With Ella with us?' Dorsey said. 'Use your head, man!'

'You're the officer,' Griffin said. 'Use yours.'

Seaver said, 'We've got to run again. Get out of this crossfire. Mount up!'

Again he helped Ella into her saddle.

Then, before Seaver could reach his own horse, a bullet nicked the haunch of Ella's horse. It squealed and broke away in a wild run westward, down the roll of the terrain. It was out of Ella's control, he knew. But, thank God, it was going in the direction he would have led.

Behind them the crossfire shifted as they gained distance, and gradually ceased as they got out of range.

Ella had a check on her spooked horse now, and Seaver caught up and took the lead.

His eyes swept the topography ahead, seeking another refuge.

To the left, where the high draw had been, there was now a huge perpendicular cliff face, impassible, but sharply cut here and there with clefts, eroded by eons of seasonal torrents that had created a canyon below.

It was into this canyon that their descent was leading them.

Across it, Seaver could see the opposite side was a wall as sheer as the bluff above.

There was no way to cross the canyon that he could see.

Behind them they could hear the Sheepeaters coming again.

Ella glanced back, then called, 'They are gaining on us!'

To their right, Seaver saw a sharp rim on the near side of the canyon, too. He could not see the lower end of it because there was a heavy growth of pine filling it. It wasn't what he had hoped to see.

They were being driven into the canyon blindly. There was no other way now to go except into it and hope to find cover from immediate attack in the trees and a possible escape route wherever the end of the canyon led.

He plunged ahead and down the steepening slope. After reaching the trees, he slowed to a walk to pick his way through the thick growth. Ella and the two men were making their way after him.

Then he burst into a narrow, dry arroyo that led through the canyon bottom toward its lower end.

He turned down it, hope rising that they had a route of escape.

The arroyo was filled with boulders, and the way was slow, but still his spirit held that they would not be caught in the bottom.

He wondered then if any of the Sheepeaters were familiar with this place. If not, they might hesitate before blindly plunging into the canyon, fearing an ambush.

Here the sandy-bottomed arroyo was wide enough that Dorsey pulled up beside him.

'They're back there,' Dorsey said. 'You can hear them thrashing around.'

'Yeah,' Seaver said.

'What about trying to stop them by ambush?'

'How many could we take, before being overrun?' Seaver said. 'Hell, there's thick trees both sides of this dry channel, They'd have us surrounded after the first shots.'

Dorsey took that in silence.

'I figure we might get our chance somewhere at the bottom end,' Seaver said.

The sound of the Sheepeaters was suddenly louder, and for a moment Seaver came close to panic.

So did Ella. She cried, 'They're closer!'

Seaver had the answer by then, as a stiff wind swept down the canyon from above, carrying sound, and continuing to blow.

'It's a strong downdraft!' he called back. But already the wind force was enough that he did not know if she heard him.

Dorsey, beside him, did. 'Like air through a bellows.'

'It can get stronger fast,' Seaver said, 'once it starts.'

'Might kick up a sandstorm,' Dorsey said. 'Could hide us.'

'Hell, it'd hide the Indians too.'

They seemed to be approaching a narrow, tree-grown exit, on each side of which rose nearly vertical walls of granite.

It was like a natural doorway.

Seaver strained to see through it, but now the increasing downdraft was picking dust from the dry arroyo and screening it from him.

'Should be open country beyond,' he shouted, turning toward Dorsey.

Dorsey nodded, but made no effort to speak.

They went through a short chasm, blinded now by the dust.

It would be a good spot to stop their pursuers, Seaver thought. A mass assault here would be impossible. He was encouraged slightly by the idea.

Then, as they emerged from the cut, the sound of the wind seemed to double. Their horses halted abruptly and refused to move.

There was a moment of clear vision, and Seaver sat there, stunned.

Barring their way was the raging torrent of a river, ripped by frothing white as far as his eye could see.

The beach on which they stood was scant yards wide, and no farther to the current's edge.

'By God,' Dorsey said. 'We're trapped.'

As the men continued to stare at the blocking water race, Ella called from behind them.

They turned and saw her point back up the canyon.

Somewhere up there, fanned by the whipping downdraft, the Sheepeaters had set fire to brush and chaparral, which in turn ignited the timber.

Now, rushing down at them with relentless speed, was a roaring front of inescapable flame.

CHAPTER SEVENTEEN

Terror in her voice, Ella said, 'Can we get into the water? Will it save us?'

Seaver turned to stare at the river again, weighing its possibilities. The violent white water of the rapids answered him.

'How?' he said. 'If we step into that, we'll be swept away in seconds and drowned in a few yards.'

But Ella's eyes were searching frantically. She said, 'There's that little cove just above us. It's almost quiet. There, where those few logs are locked in!'

Seaver looked, then moved fast toward it.

Again, his hopes were dashed.

The tiny inlet was too small to distance them from the heat of the racing flames as they closed in on the shore. The inlet had been formed by eroded soil coming down the canyon and deposited against a huge bottom-based boulder. It acted as a small breakwater of sorts, in back of which the water was calm.

The inlet was too small, and too shallow, he thought. The depth was probably barely enough to float the three logs that were there, locked together by entangled limbs.

The logs caught his attention. He called to the others, and they rushed toward him.

He said, 'If we can move those logs—'

'Move them where?' Dorsey said.

'Into the river, dammit! If they'd hold together, they'd make a raft.'

'Will they hold?' Ella said.

'Who knows? But what other chance have we got?'

He waded into the pool of calm water, which was here only knee-deep. A moment later Dorsey and Griffin were beside him.

Together they got behind the logs and shoved.

Nothing happened.

'Buried limbs, I think,' Seaver said. 'Stuck in the sand bar. Try again.'

Together they crouched so as to put their shoulders against the timbers. They seemed to give a little, then caught again.

The heat of the racing fire began to reach them. Seaver could feel it on the back of his neck.

Ella must have felt it too, because she was standing in the water now, beside him.

197

The men pushed again, their effort desperate. Ella was pushing alongside them. Still the natural raft held.

Finally, the logs moved—slightly at first, then increasingly as the clutch of the sand bottom gave way.

'Get on!' Seaver said to Ella, and as she tried to clamber aboard he gave her a shove that sent her sprawling across the logs.

'Grab hold of the branches where you can!'

She did so, and as the men felt the water deepen, they kicked with their feet to edge the raft toward the current, then hauled themselves on board just as it was caught hard by the river's force.

Seaver, the last to stop propelling, was almost too late. He came close to losing his grip.

Dorsey slid back and extended his foot to Seaver who grabbed it with both hands. Somehow Dorsey inched forward, helping Seaver to pull himself aboard.

That's another one I owe him, Seaver thought.

They were hit now by the full force of the raging white water, and each lay prone, clinging to branches or limbs wherever they could find handholds.

Seaver felt a quick blast of heat as the trees fringing the shore ignited. A moment later, he thought, and we'd have been burned to a crisp. He heard then, over the sound of wind and water, the terrible screams of their abandoned horses.

The screams seemed to go on longer than they should, and then he realized that now it was Ella that he heard, up front where the bow had gone suddenly high. He caught a glimpse of her and held his breath as the bow dropped and its weight drove it beneath the water.

For a brief moment he thought she was going to be dislodged, and wondered if he could catch her.

Somehow she held on and came up sputtering as the bow rose again, her hair wet and trailing.

His glance went beyond her, searching downriver, and all he could see was a boiling mass of white water. Worse yet, it was littered with huge, jutting boulders.

And there was no way to guide them through. No oars, not even a pole.

Directly ahead, there was a great thrusting rock.

He was shocked, knowing it was Ella up there who would take the brunt of the impact. He called out to her, 'Pull back, pull back!' but knew his words were lost in the roar of the rapids.

He began dragging himself forward, past the sprawled body of Dorsey, past that of Griffin, frantic to reach her and try to shield her with himself.

He had come only to her legs when the big

rock loomed before them, and he knew he'd lost out in whatever he was trying to do.

Then, as if by caprice, the raft swung to the right, and ground past the obstruction. A desperate desire to protect her drove him on until he lay with his body next to, and partly covering, hers.

He stayed that way as the raft pitched and tossed its way until it finally broke out at the end of those particular rapids and into a stretch of fast green water.

He didn't move, and fatigue from his efforts was only partly the cause. He found he had one arm over her shoulders, and he had no desire to relinquish her.

And she did not try to throw him off, as he half expected.

Too wrung out to care maybe, he thought.

There would be more rapids ahead, he knew, and now he studied the shoreline of the fast-moving river for a possible spot to beach if the logs could be maneuvered.

There were no places. On each side were sharp-cut banks several feet high, without even a sandbar on which to beach.

Reason told him it made no difference— there was no way to control the logs.

They would continue to be thrust onward. And once more an increasing current caused by a drop in the terrain added to their speed.

Just ahead he heard the growing sounds of another rapids.

'Slide back a ways,' he told her. 'That way, if we hit a rock head on, we'll stand a better chance.'

Ella obeyed silently, moving until her feet were near Griffin, who had lifted his head and was watching them.

Seaver moved with her, and halted as she did.

This time she turned her face toward him.

He met her eyes and saw gratitude there.

'Do you think we'll survive this river?'

'If these logs hold together, we've got a chance.'

'But the current is so swift,' she said. 'Even here.'

His hearing caught a growing rumble below them.

'Hang tight,' he said. 'There's more white water ahead.'

'Is there no end to it?' she said.

'Got to end somewhere,' he said. He moved slightly and his boot struck Griffin's head.

Seaver twisted around to look at the man.

Griffin had his face raised, staring at him. His face was hard. He said, 'That woman of yours, if she hadn't blasted that Injun chief, we wouldn't be in this trouble.'

Seaver ignored the comment and looked forward again.

They were in the breaking current now that presaged the coming rapids. The bow lifted again, then plunged, and the rush of water over them nearly swept them loose.

They came up choking and gasping, and Seaver cursed.

He had loosed his arm from Ella during the plunge, needing the grip of both hands to stay aboard and fearful of dragging her with him if he went.

Now he felt her hand groping for his. Then, as she was unable to clasp it, her fingers tightened around his wrist.

Without lifting her head, she said, 'Jon, I can't swim.'

'Makes no difference here,' he said, and they shot forward into an endless caldron of raging water. The raft struck and scraped across a submerged boulder. As it cleared, the logs that comprised it parted, one to the left, two to the right.

Seaver, clinging close to Ella, went with her on the doubled logs, along with Dorsey.

But, glancing to his left, Seaver caught sight of the lone log carrying Griffin as it shot into the rapids just as they did, but yards away. And even as he looked, the single log swung sideways and rolled, and Griffin disappeared.

The log righted itself and started racing then down the length of the rapids. But Griffin never reappeared, not even when the white water ended and once again became an unbroken, but swift-moving surface.

Seaver was scanning it for signs of Griffin's body when he caught sight of the midstream gravel bar that appeared directly ahead.

It was a low-lying island really, distant from either shore, but barren of any growth.

It fired him with a hope so that he yelled to Dorsey, 'Look ahead!'

Dorsey did so, but said, 'The current will take us around it!'

Seaver's hope fell. Dorsey was right. The chance that the splitting currents would allow them to beach was pretty slim.

But it happened.

✝   ✶   ✳

As the fire they had started raced down the canyon toward the river, the Sheepeaters watched from above. The smoke now hid from their view what was happening to the whites below.

But Tamanmo was ecstatic. 'They will burn to death,' he said.

'You will be satisfied then, Tamanmo?' a brave asked.

'Yes,' Tamanmo said. 'I will be satisfied. Although I wanted to exact my vengeance from the woman personally, I will settle for this.' He paused. 'Because we are now low on bullets for our guns.'

His braves looked at one another with expressions of relief. They were tired of the long chase.

'It will be good to get back to our women,'

one of them said.

Another said, 'It has been a worry, our women being left with little protection.' This was the one who had spoken of his concern earlier.

Tamanmo, now in a gloating mood, seemed not to notice the tone of criticism in his voice.

Another said, '*Eeyay!* I can think of another reason.'

There were chuckles among them.

They had not laughed for some time. Although they respected Tamanmo as a leader, they had become rebellious these last few days. They, none of them, were used to such sustained pursuit and fighting.

Now they watched the wind-driven fire sweep through the canyon growth and spend itself at the river edge, and were glad.

The fire had died, but some smoke lingered, when Tamanmo said, 'Come. We will see the roasted carcasses.'

He led the way through an area of lesser burn to reach the sandy arroyo bottom. On either side the scorched earth gave off heat that made them sweat, but the braves followed the chief, though with less enthusiasm. The ordeal was over, they were thinking, and they would cater to this one last whim.

They reached the end of the canyon and stopped.

For a long moment nobody spoke.

And then Tamanmo broke into a rambling,

incoherent tirade, worse than any they had yet heard.

One of the braves said, 'They got away, Tamanmo.'

With his one good eye, Tamanmo was darting glances wildly around the tiny beach. 'But how? But *how*?' he raged.

The brave pointed to the small sheltered bar. 'There,' he said. 'See where there were logs once lodged?'

'They rode the river on logs?' Tamanmo said. 'That cannot be!'

The brave did not answer him. Let him see for himself, he thought. Tamanmo, he was now certain, had gone mad. Tamanmo would have to convince himself.

The chief stepped closer to the tiny cove and stood there staring silently at the spot where the logs had lain.

He pivoted suddenly and came striding back toward the watching group.

He said then, 'We will go back to where we can climb from the canyon. We will go then down the river shore until we find them.'

'It is likely they drowned, Tamanmo.'

'It is possible they did not,' Tamanmo said. 'If that is so, they must be once more found.'

The braves looked at each other again and were silent. None of them spoke now, but there was an understanding among them. They would retrace their way up the canyon. But when they reached the point where Tamanmo

205

turned down the river, he would be alone.

They would turn the other way. The way back to the encampment, and to their poorly protected women and children.

And they would keep what ammunition they had left.

When Tamanmo went down the river shore, he would do so low on bullets.

Only the brave who had a bow and quiver of arrows would show him some help. This one would give him these weapons, just in case.

*   *   *

On the bare, isolated gravel bar, Seaver and Ella and Dorsey were marooned. They were also totally exposed to any gunfire from the shore. Their rifles were gone. Their only weapons now were the men's handguns that, strapped in their holsters, had survived the tug and lash of the river.

As had Dorsey's money belt, which he had almost immediately removed to examine. Its intricate design of folding lived up to the words of the French Canuck who'd sold it to him. The currency was dry.

The westering sun slowly dried their clothing, before it sank from view. Exhausted, they slept, huddled against the night's cold, Ella between the two men.

The next morning Seaver could not judge the distance they had covered during the river ride.

But he feared it wasn't enough. He eyed the shore almost continuously, fearing the worst.

Once he said to Dorsey, 'Can you swim?'

And Dorsey said, 'Some.'

He turned then to look behind them at the milling turmoil of water that blocked them from the other, far more distant shore. To attempt a crossing there would be suicidal. They would drown.

He turned back to the nearer shore. It would take a strong swimmer even to reach that, he thought.

He was strong and he could swim. But he was not proficient at it, had done little of it since boyhood.

And if he made it, what then? Ella would still be stranded in midriver.

At that moment, he heard Ella cry out.

'There he is. In that clearing!'

Seaver and Dorsey looked.

Across from them was the Sheepeater chief, mounted and staring back.

He appeared to be alone.

The range was too far for accurate revolver fire, but not for the rifle they saw in the hands of the Indian.

There was no cover, no concealment on the barren gravel bar.

We are totally exposed to his bullets, Seaver thought. It all depends on what kind of a marksman he is with that one eye.

As they watched, the Sheepeater

dismounted, lay prone, and took a long time sighting on them.

Seaver said, 'Try to keep moving.'

Just as they did so, the Indian fired.

He missed.

Seaver looked and saw him sighting again. So did Dorsey and Ella.

They kept moving this direction and that, dispersing, tense with the expectation of a bullet.

The Indian fired five times.

If we could only dig a trench, Seaver thought. But the gravel was hard packed to the density of pavement, and they had nothing to dig with but their bare hands.

The shooting ceased abruptly.

They looked across the current and saw the Indian stand, stare at them, then throw down his weapon.

'By God!' Seaver said. 'I think he's out of ammo.'

'Let's hope,' Dorsey said. 'It was only chance that kept us from getting hit.'

'Chance and his bad eye.' Seaver glanced at Ella as he said it. He was surprised at the fixed, hard look on her face. It was the first time since she had mutilated the chief that she did not show remorse for her action.

Suddenly it occurred to him that the Indian had a horse. A horse could be made to swim that current and carry Ella back to shore. If Seaver could get the horse.

He started for the water's edge. Ella and Dorsey stared at him.

'I'm going to swim for it,' he said.

'Why?' Ella said.

'I'm thinking he has no bullets left. If I can get over there, armed, and take his horse—'

'What good will that do?' Dorsey said.

'I'll bring the horse over here and Ella can ride it back to the shore.'

Seaver slipped into the water, and reached out with long, powerful strokes, beating slowly ahead even as the current swept him downriver. He was far down, out of sight of the Indian when he finally reached the shore. He was blowing hard, sucking for air. Minutes passed before he caught his breath, and then he began making his way up the shore. He loosened his holster strap for easy weapon reach when it was needed.

Find the Indian, get the horse. He kept repeating that order to himself, to fight against the exhaustion of his swim.

He got to where he could see the lower end of the gravel bar, and knew he was close to the clearing where he'd last sighted the Sheepeater chief.

The Indian would have seen him enter the water, and would be on watch to see if he'd survived the crossing.

There was only a thin fringe of the pines screening him from the clearing when an arrow came from nowhere and drove quivering into a trunk a foot away from his chest.

He jumped back into hiding.

He's out of bullets for sure, Seaver thought. *But he has a bow.*

So now it's my handgun against his arrows.

Where is he? And where is the horse?

Seaver studied the direction from where he guessed the arrow had come, then skirted the clearing, slipping as quietly as he could through the growth, knowing his risk, but desperate enough to take chances.

They saw each other at the same moment.

The Indian had an arrow already nocked in his bowstring. He had heard him coming.

Seaver had his revolver in his fist.

They shot together.

Even at that short distance, the chief's eyesight betrayed him.

The arrow missed, the bullet did not.

The chief was driven back, to fall face up. Blood spurted from a hole just below his breastbone.

Gut shot. Seaver knew he was a dying man.

He started toward the body, just as the Indian's pony, spooked by the close gunfire, burst by on a wild run.

Seaver made a futile grab at a trailing rein, and missed.

He swore, as he ran after it. Without the horse there would be no escape from the island for Ella.

In its panic the mount ran toward the river,

then stopped abruptly at the shore.

Seaver lurched after it, and this time caught the rein. Fearful it might break away again, he threw himself up to straddle its back.

Across the current he could see Ella, with Dorsey, watching him. He turned the horse upriver, and rode it to where he had allowed for the current's downward push. He drove it to enter the water then. The pony seemed well trained and, after an initial balk, began a frantic swim, though Seaver had to rein heavily to keep it from turning with the pull of the current.

Then, as the current swept them to a point even with the top end of the sand bar, he saw it was still many yards away.

Too many, he thought. Had he misjudged the velocity of the water?

They were still several feet from the bar as they neared its toe.

The Indian pony seemed to sense the landfall was going to be missed. Seaver pressed his heels hard into its flanks, felt its final desperate effort, and that was what it took.

The animal's hoofs dug into the last few feet of the hard sand spit, and hauled them ashore.

He slipped from the mount's back, but held the rein.

Dorsey and Ella came running to him.

He looked at Ella then.

'Your turn,' he said.

'Can I make it?'

He saw her worry, and said, 'Going that direction, you can't miss the shore.'

'Is the Indian dead?'

'He's dead. I gut-shot him.'

'There may be others.'

'If there were, they'd have come running at the sound of my shot.'

She still looked dubious. 'I'd kill myself, rather than be blinded.'

He unbuckled his gun belt and adjusted it around her waist.

They were both silent as he did this.

He boosted her onto the pony's back then, and she grasped at its mane to hold on. He led it to the current's edge and handed her the rein. Their eyes met for a moment, and he said, 'You can do it, Ella.' He paused. 'And when you get there, keep the horse if you can.'

Her face was grim, but she nodded. He slapped the pony's haunch.

And again, reluctantly, the obedient mount began to swim.

Dorsey said, 'Hell of a chance.'

'Did you have a better idea?'

Dorsey was silent for a moment before he spoke.

'No.'

'Well then.'

They stood side by side, watching as the current carried the woman on the horse out of their sight around a slight bend.

'You said you could swim,' Seaver said.

212

'Some, yes.'

'Let's go.'

Dorsey stared at the current, but made no move.

Seaver got in the water and headed across. He glanced back, and Dorsey was following.

Two thirds of the way across, and far down the shoreline, Seaver began to tire. He had already crossed once, and a second time on the Indian horse. He rolled over to look for Dorsey, and saw the man sinking, his arms no longer flailing.

With an effort he got himself flipped around and swam back to grasp a fistful of Dorsey's hair, just as he went down. He treaded water with his legs and lifted Dorsey's head high enough for him to breathe.

He set out then on his side, stroking with only his right arm, tugging Dorsey along with a grip on his wrist.

They finally reached the shore, and lay there gasping, neither inclined to move. Ella and the horse were nowhere to be seen.

Then, from higher up the river, they heard the shot.

'Ella!' Seaver said.

He made it to his feet, staggering toward the sound.

Behind him Dorsey struggled to his feet to follow.

What the hell went on? Seaver thought. Why didn't she wait for us where she landed?

She had to be in trouble.

He was running wildly now, beating his way through the growth.

He burst into the clearing where he had left the body of the Indian chief.

He was shocked to see the body in a different position, clutching the bow in a death grip.

A dropped arrow pointed roughly across the clearing. Looking there Seaver saw Ella sitting.

She held Seaver's revolver limply at her side.

He moved toward her, and she looked up at him dully and said, 'He's dead—now.'

'Now?' Seaver said. 'He was still alive when you got here?'

'Enough to put an arrow in that bow.'

'I heard the shot.'

'I shot him,' she said. 'It was him or me.'

He was silent.

'Do you understand?' she said, and her voice grew hard as she said it again. '*It was him or me.*'

CHAPTER EIGHTEEN

They followed the river downstream, Ella riding the Indian pony, the two men walking.

She was silent, and Seaver thought that her killing of the Sheepeater chief weighed heavy on her.

But glancing at her later, he noted that a

hardness had replaced the tormented expression he had often seen on her face since the time she had first wounded the Indian.

She has come to an acceptance of how things are, he thought, of how things happen regardless of how much we might wish otherwise.

He was glad she was making peace with the situation. Such acceptance was the only way she could live with what she had been forced to do.

He knew this well, from his own experiences.

Their final flight from the Sheepeaters, with their dash through the canyon and the wild river ride, had lost them the trail, and for another day they wandered, guided only by the sun.

When they finally emerged from the wilderness, Seaver guessed they were not too distant from the way he had earlier taken in his pursuit of Pandre.

He judged they were north of it somewhat, which was fortunate, because they came upon a small herd of grazing cattle, and beyond they could see ranch buildings.

Hunger and exhaustion plagued them now, and their pace was slow, even though they had a desire to hurry.

It was slow enough that when they reached the ranch yard, a man and a woman waited on the porch. The man held a rifle partly raised.

Seaver led the way up to them, seeing the

half-afraid look on the woman's middle-aged face and the searching eyes of the man. Then the woman's glance went to Ella, still astride the Indian pony, and her worried features eased. She seemed about to speak, but her husband held up a palm in front of her and stopped her.

The man looked at the pony.

He said, 'Injun horse, ain't it? You folks have a run-in?'

Seaver nodded. 'Sort of.'

Dorsey spoke up. 'We could use a meal. We can pay.'

The man was silent, and his eyes went from Dorsey to Ella, and he gave her a studying look.

He lowered his rifle and said, 'Light, ma'am, if you have such a wish.'

Dorsey was there to catch her as she slid from the mount.

'Tie the pony to the rack there,' the rancher said. 'I'll tend to it in a bit.'

Dorsey did so.

The woman said, 'You folks come on in. I'll throw a quick meal together to get you started.'

The meal was one of heated leftovers, served apologetically by the woman.

'It's fine,' Ella told her. 'We ate nothing yesterday.'

The men said nothing.

Seaver was a little surprised at the lack of questioning by the couple. Momentarily he put

216

it off to courtesy while they were satisfying their hunger.

But even when they had finished and sat back replete, again thanking their hosts, the latter were strangely uninquisitive. And when Dorsey took currency from his money belt and laid it on the table, the rancher did not reach for it, although he gave it a fascinated stare.

Dorsey said, 'Is there a town anywhere about?'

The rancher hesitated, then said, 'Place called Red Pine ain't far.'

'How far?' Seaver said.

'Ten miles south,' the woman said.

The man looked quickly at her, as if he didn't like her answering.

'Long walk,' Seaver said.

Dorsey said, 'You got a couple of horses you can sell?'

'This is a small ranch,' the man said. 'But I may have one I could let you have.'

'Still a long walk for one of us,' Seaver said.

'Big old gelding,' the man said. 'Slow, but strong enough you could ride him double, one of you men and the lady.'

The woman had her eyes on her husband, as if searching his mind as he spoke.

She said now, 'That Injun pony looks hard used. Be best if you stayed the night here, ate a good dinner and breakfast, and set off fresh come morning.'

'She's right,' the rancher said. 'That Injun

horse can't take much more without some feed and rest.'

Ella said, 'Your offer is very kind. And I, for one, would gladly accept it.'

'Is that agreed then?' the rancher said.

Seaver looked at Dorsey, and Dorsey nodded.

'Agreed,' Seaver said.

'Come on then,' the man said. 'I'll tend to the pony, and show you the gelding.'

'By the way,' the woman said, 'we're the Jeffersons.'

Seaver and Dorsey nodded, then exchanged glances with each other and with Ella. They seemed to share a mutual thought, that the Jeffersons did not inquire *their* names. It was as if they already knew.

Outside, a young ranchhand appeared as they approached the small rustic corral.

Jefferson said, 'This is Jake, works for me.'

He was an intelligent-looking youth, Seaver thought.

'Jake,' Jefferson said, 'get that Injun pony, tied there to the rack, and feed, water, and put him up at the stable.'

'Yes, sir,' Jake said, and hurried off to take care of it.

'Only full-time employee I got,' Jefferson said.

There were only four horses in the corral.

'That big black gelding is the one I'd sell,' the rancher said. 'Got fifteen years on him, but

218

he'll get you there.'

'How much?' Dorsey said.

'Fifty bucks, with an old beat-up saddle and bridle included.'

'Done.'

Jefferson took the money, then said, 'You can maybe trade him in Red Pine, and the Injun pony too. Get yourself other mounts for where you're going.'

'Sure,' Dorsey said.

'Well, reckon you folks might like to rest up some while the wife fixes up a sure-enough supper.'

'I would,' Ella said.

'We got a spare room in the house to put you up for the night, ma'am. And the menfolk can bed down on the porch. I'll rustle up some blankets.'

'That's very kind, Mr Jefferson,' Ella said.

'Glad we're able to do it,' the rancher said.

*   *   *

On the ranch-house porch, Seaver slept the sleep of the exhausted.

Only once during the night did he even partly awaken: a brief sound came from over near the tack room. Injun pony feeling restless in a stable, he thought, and went back to sleep.

In the morning, Mrs Jefferson served them a real ranch breakfast, the first good one they'd had since they'd left Kelly's mining camp.

Then the rancher led them out to the corral and personally got the black horse, took it to the tack shed, and threw on it a worn and torn saddle.

'Ain't much,' he said. 'But it'll do.'

Seaver kept thinking that he could have said the same thing when they got the black from the corral. There was something there that bothered him, but he couldn't remember what it was.

A few minutes later the ranch couple waved them off.

Ella waved back from her position behind Seaver on the black.

Dorsey rode the Indian pony.

'Seemed like nice people,' Ella said. 'Real western courtesy, I thought, not to pry into what we were doing here.'

'Yeah,' Seaver said. 'Some of these folks are like that.'

*   *   *

The town was a small ranching and mining center, though neither mines nor ranches were close enough to be visible from Red Pine. It was there to offer supplies to either.

Near noon, the three approached Red Pine's dirt main street, lined with board-front structures.

'Hell of a quiet town,' Seaver said.

'I don't expect there's much excitement here.

Except maybe on Saturday nights,' Dorsey said.

'I guess that's why they keep a marshal on the payroll.' Seaver nodded toward a sign on one of the fronts.

A little way down the street was a small saloon, with a single horse hitched to the rack before it.

It caught Seaver's eye and held it.

He said in an aside to Dorsey, not turning his head, 'That roan horse have a familiar look to you?'

'It does so,' Dorsey said.

Seaver said, 'I recollect now there was one less horse in that corral this morning.'

'That kid, Jake, could have ridden it in last night.'

'My thinking exactly,' Seaver said. 'Matter of fact, I heard some movement that woke me up.'

'Our courteous friends, the Jeffersons, could have sent him,' Dorsey said.

'Why?' Ella said.

'We just passed a marshal's office,' Seaver said.

'Our good friends figure to share some bounty money with him, I'm guessing,' Dorsey said. 'On me.'

'How would they know?' Ella said. 'About you—about us?'

'Look ahead, ma'am. This side of the livery stable.'

221

She looked and saw the lettering on a structure just beyond.

'*Red Pine Record*,' she read.

'Sounds like a newspaper,' Seaver said.

'There's your answer, ma'am,' Dorsey said. 'Your story and mine are likely front-page stuff in a lot of places by now. And those Jeffersons saw us together, sent word in.'

'They seemed like such nice people.'

'In my present line of work, those are the kind I have to watch out for,' Dorsey said.

His words caused Ella to frown.

Seaver noted that and thought, *She doesn't like to think of him being a bank robber*. It bothered him that he shared her feeling. Going through danger together tended to form a bond between people.

Seaver said, 'Keep riding to the livery stable at the end of the street. If we can get good horses—'

'It isn't you two they're after,' Dorsey said.

Ella looked at him, still frowning. Then she waited to hear Seaver's reaction.

Seaver said, 'Dammit, keep riding!'

Dorsey shrugged. 'Your decision,' he said.

A few paces on, his eyes went up to study the high false fronts on either side.

'Drop back,' he said to Seaver and Ella, mounted on the black.

'Why?'

'Just caught a glint from a roof,' he said tightly. 'Goddammit, drop back!'

Seaver swept a glance along the line of roofs. He saw a couple of rifle barrels showing and halted.

Ella saw them too.

'They'll kill him!' she cried.

Seaver held the gelding still.

'Do something!' she said harshly.

He said to Dorsey then, 'Put up your hands! You're worth more to them alive than dead.'

'You're right,' Dorsey said, and raised his hands.

One of the rifles fired, and his left hand spurted blood.

He dropped both hands, reached for his gun, and shot the rifleman off the roof. The man came sliding down the gable slope behind the false facade and dropped into a narrow space between the buildings.

He lay there, moaning.

Dorsey kicked the Indian pony into a run. Two or three other rifles opened fire as he ran the gauntlet and reached some trees.

'That changes things,' Seaver said.

'But how?'

He made no answer as the gunfire brought people into the street behind them.

One, wearing a star, came running toward them, a six-gun in his hand.

'Stop right there!' he shouted to Seaver.

'I am stopped,' Seaver said, twisting to look at him.

He was a young man with hard-tempered

223

face. 'Smart bastard, huh?' he said.

'Smart enough to stay put,' Seaver said.

The marshal halted abreast of them, seeing the dust at the end of the street where Dorsey had just disappeared.

'What you doing, riding with him?' he said. He held his gun tilted up at Seaver as he spoke.

'It's a long story,' Seaver said.

'That Bart Dorsey just got away?'

'Yeah. But put that damn gun up. I figure you got the recent news here, maybe. I'm Jon Seaver, and this is Miss Ella Gordon.'

'In that case, I'll want to talk to you later,' the marshal said. 'Right now I got a horse waiting, saddled, at the stable. Dorsey is my priority.'

'Kind of passed you by, Marshal.'

'Dammit! I was in the privy. But he won't get away. Don't neither of you leave town,' the lawman said.

He went running toward the livery. A couple of minutes later he reappeared mounted and rode off fast in the direction Dorsey had gone.

Some of the townspeople had come close.

Seaver said, 'There's a wounded man between those buildings.'

Most of them moved rapidly over to see. One came away running and went back up the street, throwing the word 'doctor' over his shoulder.

One of the townsmen had remained. He said, 'I'm George Raitt, mayor here.'

224

'Jon Seaver,' Seaver said.

'I read about you in the newspaper,' Raitt said. He tipped his hat to Ella. 'You must be Miss Gordon, I presume.'

She nodded. Her mind seemed to be on Dorsey's escape.

'Be best if you wait at the hotel,' Raitt said. 'Marshal Thayer will want a word with you.'

'When?'

'Why, when he gets back,' Raitt said. 'Meanwhile, our local editor will be eager to interview you about your recent experience, as would I.' He paused. 'Miss Gordon's abduction, I hear, has made the news all over the country. And the Salmon City bank robbery to a lesser extent. With nothing further known for nearly two weeks.'

'This old horse needs rest,' Seaver said.

Raitt motioned a man to him. 'Take the black here to the livery. Tell Sam I'll stand good for its keep.'

'Yes, Mr Raitt,' the man said and, as Seaver and Ella dismounted, led the horse away.

They fell in beside Raitt as he went back past the marshal's office to the single-story hotel.

Ella's mood remained subdued.

*   *   *

The Indian pony had carried Dorsey the ten miles from Jefferson's ranch to Red Pine already that morning. And Marshall Thayer's

225

horse was fresh.

Dorsey soon heard its hoofbeats behind him.

Looking back he saw the rider, saw the glint of his star, and felt the finality of his robbery career closing in.

His hand was bleeding badly. But the beginning of the end, he thought, was when he shot that citizen sniper on the roof back there.

It was the first time he'd shot anyone in his role as a bank robber. True, he had often threatened with his gun, but he had never used it.

That he hadn't was mostly because he hadn't needed to. A matter of luck, for which he couldn't take much credit, he told himself.

Until now, though, he'd accepted the fact that sooner or later it would happen. It was something he lived with. Compared with his part in that early Indian village massacre, it seemed a minor burden.

He felt surprise now that it bothered him so much. After all, the sniper had shot him first. He returned fire in self-defense.

Still, it was an act he wished he had not committed.

For some reason, the image of Ella suddenly intruded on his thoughts. And he knew his regret was due to her. A remorse over what might have been, had he not become what he was.

This train of thought was abruptly broken as

226

the lawman drew close enough to fire a shot at him.

Dorsey halted the pony, turned it to face the marshal, and raised his hands. The pain in his left one now bordered on the unbearable.

Marshal Thayer slowed his mount and came on cautiously.

'Lost your nerve, eh?' he said.

'Maybe,' Dorsey said. 'But mostly, I've lost a lot of blood.'

He wasn't lying. Blood ran down his arm and dripped from his elbow.

Thayer came carefully close until he could reach Dorsey's gun and draw it from its holster. He shoved it in his belt and backed off again before he spoke.

'The famed Bart Dorsey,' he said.

Dorsey had dropped his hands after his gun was taken. He said, 'Is it all right if I wrap my neckerchief around this bleeding?'

'I reckon.' The marshal was still keeping his weapon fisted. 'Get ahead of me and head back for town.'

'Sure thing,' Dorsey said.

'You shot a citizen,' Thayer said. 'I ought to blow your damn head off—'

'Don't do it,' Dorsey said. 'I'm worth double to you alive.'

'I know about the bounty.'

'I'm sure you do.'

'I heard you was once a army officer,' the marshal said.

'Yeah, once.'

'Fell a hell of a long way, didn't you?'

Dorsey gave the comment some thought before he answered ironically, 'Not as long a fall as you might think.'

* * *

As they rode into town, people on the street watched their approach.

Thayer yelled at the first one he got near to, 'Get the doctor down to the jail. I got a man here I damn well don't want to bleed to death!'

The man said, 'Doc is busy. Trying to save Joe Karnes, got shot off the roof by that bastard you got there. Let him bleed, I say!'

'Then you tell Doc to get the hell down to the jail as soon as he can,' Thayer said.

The man scowled, spit in the direction of Dorsey, but turned reluctantly to do as he was bid.

Thayer escorted Dorsey to the jail office, and herded him inside and into a cell.

Dorsey sat on the bunk, squeezing his neckerchief around his wounded hand.

Thayer left, came back in a couple of minutes, and tossed a towel in through the bars. He didn't say a word, but he looked worried.

Even in his pain, Dorsey seemed amused by that. 'You better get a medico in here pretty soon, or it's going to cost you.'

'I got it in mind,' Thayer said. 'I'm going after him myself now.'

He was gone awhile, and when he came back, leading the doctor, Dorsey said, 'I thought you'd forgot me.'

'I'd damn well like to,' the marshal said harshly. 'You put Joe Karnes in bad shape, what with the fall from the roof and all. He may not live.'

Dorsey's face turned somber.

'I'm sorry it happened.'

The doctor was a gaunt, middle-aged man, with a no nonsense manner.

He said, 'You'll be a hell of a lot sorrier if he dies.'

'What does that mean?' Dorsey said.

'He's well liked in this town,' Thayer said.

The doctor pulled Dorsey's right hand grasp free from the neckerchief wrapping and unwound it roughly. 'And a personal friend of mine,' he said.

Dorsey gritted his teeth, but said nothing.

'There's going to be trouble enough, anyway,' Thayer said. 'Word is getting around.'

'What trouble?' Dorsey said.

'Rope trouble.'

'You ought to let them have him,' the doctor said.

'He's worth five hundred more alive,' the marshal said.

'Worth five hundred to see him lynched,' the

doctor said.

'Not for me, it ain't,' Thayer said.

The doctor seemed not to hear. His concentration on the wound had taken over. He opened his medical bag and took out instruments, antiseptic, swabs, and some metal clips.

As he cleaned the wound he said, 'Rifle bullet nicked an artery. Been a six-gun slug it'd likely blown off your whole hand.'

He worked then for nearly half an hour in silence.

When he was done, he stepped back and said, 'I should have sewed you up with harness twine and a coarse needle.'

'He going to be all right, Doc?' Thayer said. His concern was obvious.

That seemed to irritate the doctor, and he said, 'Money mean that much to you, Marshal?'

'When you work for sixty dollars a month,' Thayer said, 'it weighs heavy.'

'Is that so? Then let me ask you, did you shake him down for a hideout gun?'

The marshal showed chagrin. 'You feel one on him?'

'Not a gun,' Doc said. 'But I felt a money belt under that bloody shirt.'

'I'd best check it out.'

Doc headed for the door. 'Wait till I'm out of here. If he goes to trial, there could be questions I don't want to know about.'

Dorsey said, '*If* I go to trial?'

'Exactly,' the doctor said, and exited from the cell.

* * *

It was the mayor, Raitt, who brought the word of Dorsey's capture to Ella and Seaver at the hotel.

'He has a wound,' Ella said.

'We've got a doctor looking after it,' Raitt said. 'But I still don't understand your traveling in his company.'

'I want to see him,' Ella said.

'I'm baffled, Miss Gordon,' Raitt said. 'He is a wanted bank robber. Not the kind of company I'd expect you to keep.'

Seaver said, 'I can explain it in part. We met up with him in a chance encounter on the trail. We became allies when we were attacked by a band of Sheepeater Indians. You might say we saved each other's lives.'

'And because of that, you became friends?'

'Close to it,' Seaver said.

Ella was up and walking toward the door.

Seaver started to follow. He said to Raitt, 'You coming with us?'

Raitt said, 'It's better that I don't. It wouldn't be politically wise for me, you understand? The citizens here who made me mayor, well, they are mostly friends of the man Bart Dorsey shot.' He paused, then said in a low voice, 'Joe Karnes is dead.'

'Damn!' Seaver said, and exited quickly after Ella.

As they approached the site of the jail and marshal's office, they could see a gathering of townsfolks in the street before it.

'What's going on?' Ella asked.

'Friends of the man Bart shot, I reckon.'

'What do they want?'

'I'd guess they want to hang him.'

'Good God!' she said. 'They can't!'

He was silent.

'Can they?' she cried.

'The man he shot just died,' Seaver said.

A moment later they saw something else.

Bart Dorsey's body hung by its neck from a jutting flagpole above the door of the marshal's porchless office.

*　　*　　*

Inside the office, the marshal sat at his desk, leaning forward with his head on his folded arms.

As they entered, he raised a solemn face. 'I tried to stop them,' he said.

'Not too hard, I reckon,' Seaver said.

'Listen,' Thayer said, 'I didn't want this to happen.'

Ella said in a shaken voice, 'He deserved a lawful trial.'

'I tried, believe me. Ma'am, not being able to turn him over live, that cost me half the bounty

232

money.'

Seaver said, 'He wore a money belt.'

Thayer looked perturbed, then said, 'You know about that?'

'I know.'

Thayer did not speak for a moment. Then he said, 'Listen, you'll need stage fare to take the lady back to Silver City.'

'You trying to buy my silence?'

'We could split the couple hundred was in his belt.'

Seaver gave him a skeptical look.

'Look,' Thayer said, 'he had accomplices when he robbed that bank in Salmon City. The news report said they stole about fifteen hundred. They must have shared the take. Dorsey told me the others were killed back there in the wild area. He told me their money was lost with them.'

'Reckon it was,' Seaver said. 'But, as leader, Dorsey could have taken a double share.'

Thayer said, 'Jefferson's messenger said he paid with bank bills for the black horse and a saddle. That would account for some spent.'

Seaver was thinking. Dorsey had spent liberally for them all in Kelly's camp. And fifty for the horse and gear. Take that from Dorsey's double split of the loot: Seven hundred, less maybe two hundred. That'd leave five hundred.

He said, 'No wonder you didn't put up a fight when that mob out there came for him.'

'Had nothing to do with it,' Thayer said. 'I couldn't stop them without shooting. And I have to live with these people. They're the ones keep me in this job. A lawman's job is part politics, friend.'

Seaver exchanged glances with Ella. He saw that the remark had its effect on her. As it did on him.

'Politics,' he aid. 'Yes, I guess that's so.' He paused. 'I'll take two hundred to get us where we're going. And you see he gets buried proper, hear?'

When they left the jail, the body of Dorsey was still hanging in the noose. Ella quickly averted her eyes, which were filled with tears. As they neared the hotel, she spoke, 'Fifteen hundred dollars, split four ways, and for that he's dead?'

Seaver was silent.

CHAPTER NINETEEN

The weekly stage out of Red Pine was a day away, and Seaver and Ella attended the burial.

They were the only ones who did, except for a pair of boot-hill gravediggers who stood by as the undertaker parroted a few meaningless phrases.

Ella cried, and Seaver gave what was the real eulogy.

'He was a soldier again, when he was needed,' he said.

234

*   *   *

Four days later the stage pulled into Silver City.

Sheriff Big Jim Halloran was there on the Idaho Hotel porch, waiting for them.

'Word was wired down from Red Pine that you was on your way,' he said. 'How are you, Ella?'

'Well enough, Sheriff.'

'I guess I picked the right man to send after you,' Halloran said.

She gave him a tired smile. But there was an enthusiasm in her voice when she said, 'You most certainly did, Sheriff!'

He gave her a curious stare, and his face fell a little, as if her enthusiasm bothered him.

His annoyance caused him to turn to Seaver and say, 'Well, Seaver, you've earned the big reward. And that's what you went for.'

'You know better,' Seaver said.

Ella frowned. 'And so do I.'

Halloran was silent. He was smart enough not to contest her feeling at this time.

Instead, he said, 'Ella, I took your clothing and valises from the hotel room for safekeeping in my office.'

'Thank you,' she said. 'I'll be taking a room again for a night or two. I need time to recover.'

'I'll have your gear brought up,' he said.

He looked sharply then at Seaver. Although

he didn't yet know the particulars of the rescue, he knew there had been prolonged contact between Seaver and Ella.

How deep did it go, and what form did it take? he wondered. Halloran had not really been close to Ella Gordon before her abduction, but he had considered her a likely candidate for his affections.

And now, appraising what might be between Seaver and her, he was overcome by full-blown jealousy.

'And you,' Halloran said to Seaver. 'It'll take a little time to get your reward qualified and sent here.'

Ella looked at the sheriff and said, 'It would be hard to find a better man for a job as deputy.'

Seaver, as well as Halloran, showed surprise.

'Seems like you've had a change of mind about me being fit to be a lawman,' Seaver said.

'I understand now, Jon,' she said. 'I understand because I was drawn into war myself.'

Halloran said, 'You?'

She nodded. 'Against Sheepeater Indians.'

'What?'

'I wounded,' she said. 'And finally I killed.'

'*You?*' Halloran said again.

'It was like Jon said it was with him. It wasn't my wish to take someone's life. I did what I had to do.'

She paused, then said, 'God help me.'